BRAIN STORM PUZZLES and CHALLENGES for BRIGHT KIDS

First published by Red Panda, an imprint of Westland Books, a division of Nasadiya Technologies Private Limited, in 2022

No. 269/2B, First Floor, 'Irai Arul', Vimalraj Street, Nethaji Nagar, Alapakkam Main Road, Maduravoyal, Chennai 600095

ISBN: 9789395767101

10 9 8 7 6 5

Book design by New Media Line Creations, New Delhi

Images sourced from Shutterstock

Printed at Nutech Print Services Pvt. Ltd

1 Find the unique image that appears only once.

2 Combine the two pieces of the puzzle below, to create a whole square. Identify which square (from a to d) is the correct one.

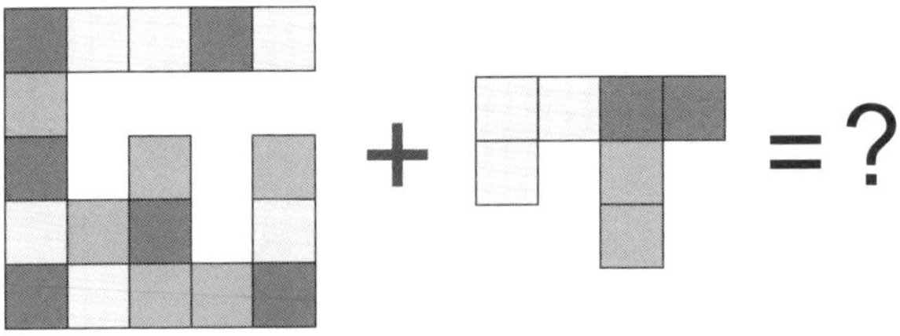

a)

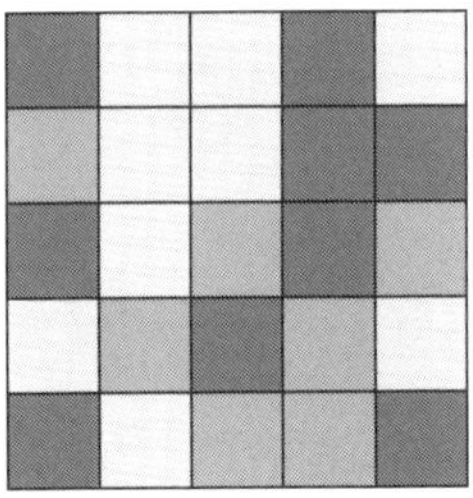

b)

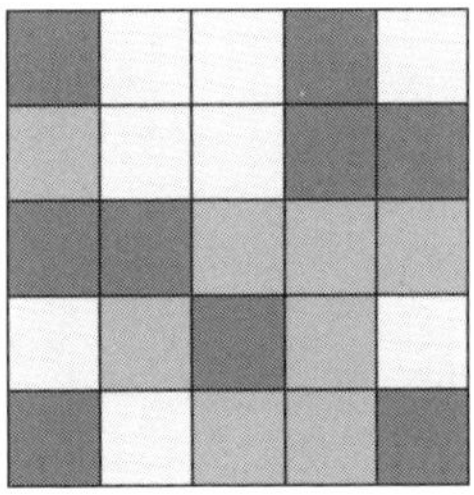

c)

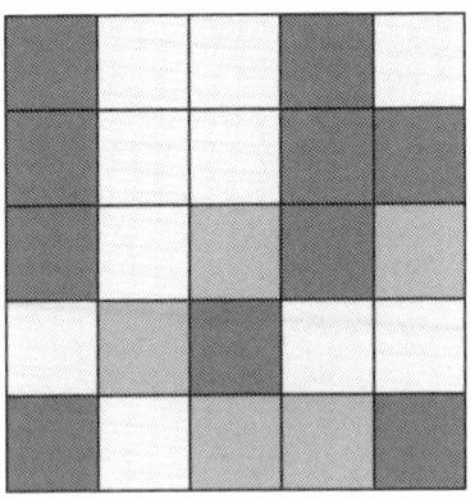

d)

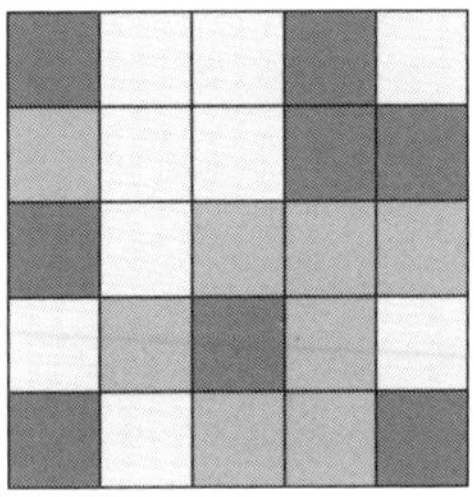

3 Which souvenir did the tourist buy?

4 Match the statements in the bubble with their right answers.

1. Monkey
2. Edward Jenner
3. Wireless Fidelity
4. Jellyfish
5. Light
6. Bhaskara
7. Rakesh Sharma
8. Dog
9. Heart
10. Sound
11. Graham Bell
12. Kalpana Chawla
13. Wireless Firewall
14. Starfish
15. Aryabhata
16. Liver

A. The first animal to go to space
B. A fish with no skeleton
C. WiFi stands for
D. The father of vaccination
E. This travels the fastest
F. The organ that purifies blood
G. The first Indian in space
H. The first Indian satellite

5 Can you guess the idiom?

1

2

3

4

5

6

6 Find the two identical gears.

7 Use your addition and subtraction skills to complete the fun maths puzzle.

		☐	−	7	=	2		☐		
						+		+		
				5		☐		1		
				−		=		=		
				☐	+	7	=	9		
				=						
		☐	−	☐	=	5				
		−				+				
5	+	☐	=	9		☐				
		=				=				
☐	−	4	=	3		6	−	☐	=	1
				+				+		
				☐				3		
				=				=		
				6	+	☐	=	8		

8

The Khannas are helping collect the garbage left by irresponsible hikers in the forest.

Search the objects in the trash cans, in the picture.
And sort the trash by labelling each can.

9 Hidden in the image below are 10 snowflake patterns, similar to the one in the box. Find them.

10 Help the little ghost get out of the maze. Make a path by drawing a line through the boxes that add up to **8**, **12** or **18**.

11 + 1	10 + 2	4 + 8	6 + 6 = 12	11 + 3	
9 + 9	17 + 2			13 + 3	2 + 6
3 + 5	6 + 2	15 + 4	7 + 3	7 + 1	17 + 1
18 + 1	12 + 6	1 + 7	3 + 16	5 + 3	8 + 7
12 + 4	1 + 8	4 + 4	5 + 5	13 + 5	10 + 7
16 + 1	3 + 8	7 + 11	8 + 10	14 + 4	11 + 3

11 Help the racing car reach the finish line. Find the correct directions from the options given in the box below.

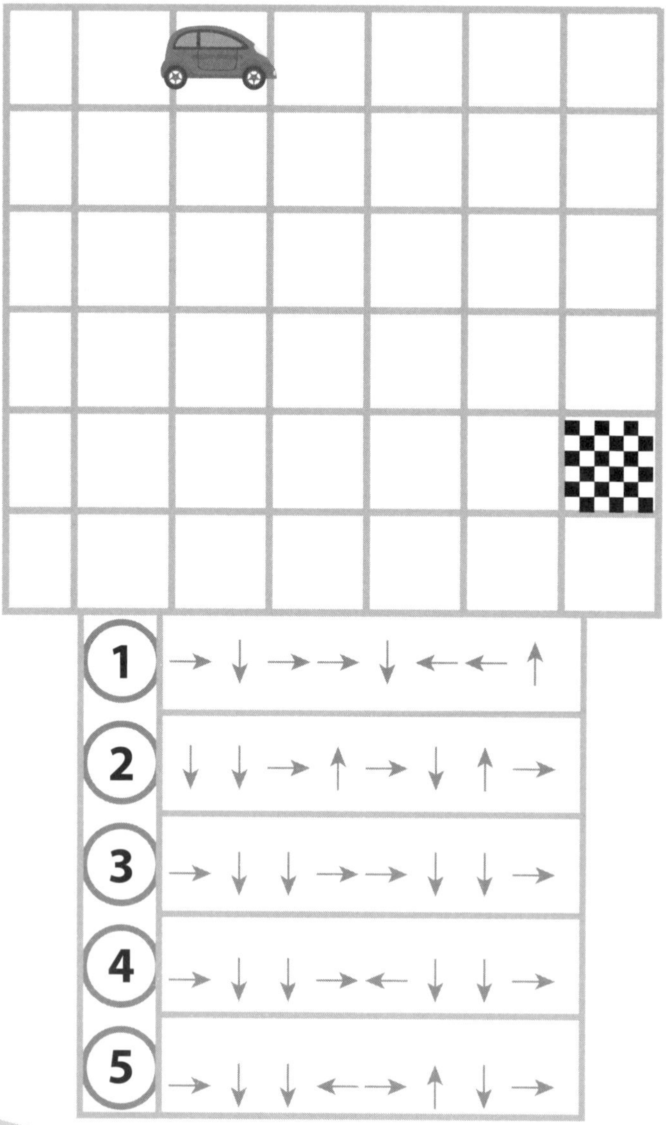

1. → ↓ → → ↓ ← ← ↑
2. ↓ ↓ → ↑ → ↓ ↑ →
3. → ↓ ↓ → → ↓ ↓ →
4. → ↓ ↓ → ← ↓ ↓ →
5. → ↓ ↓ ← → ↑ ↓ →

12 Choose the correct article for each word.

○ a
○ an
mirror 

○ a
○ an
bee 

○ a
○ an
invitation 

○ a
○ an
unicorn 

○ a
○ an
jacket 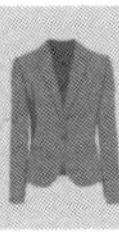

○ a
○ an
frog 

○ a
○ an
hourglass 

○ a
○ an
comb 

○ a
○ an
igloo 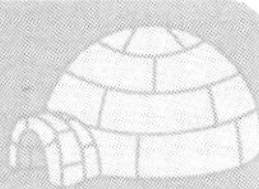

○ a
○ an
university 

○ a
○ an
dog 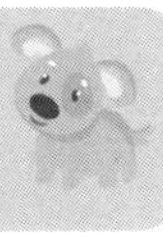

○ a
○ an
bear 

○ a
○ an
umbrella 

○ a
○ an
eagle 

○ a
○ an
horse 

○ a
○ an
soap 

13 Move three matchsticks in each set to make five triangles.

1

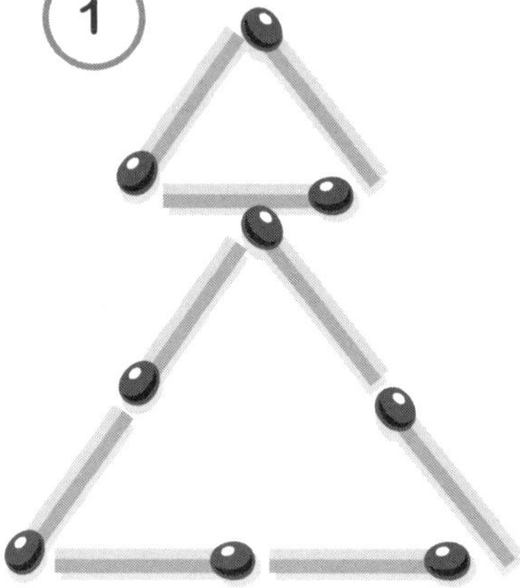

2

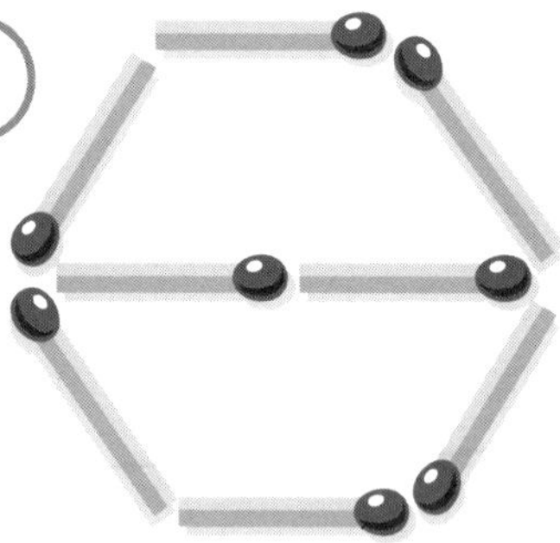

3

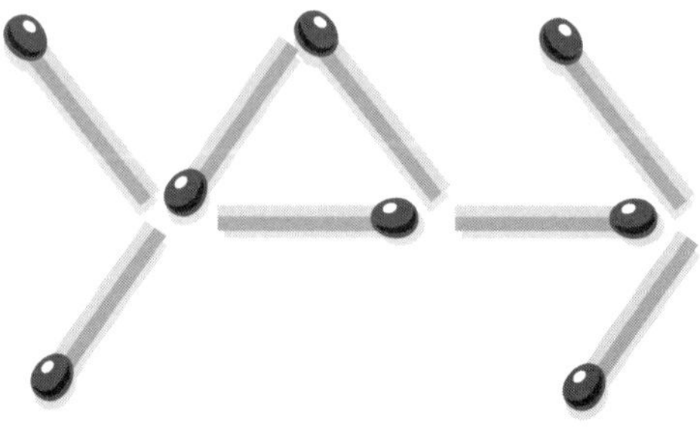

14 Hidden in this word puzzle are the names of 10 national parks in India. Look for them vertically, horizontally and diagonally.

S	S	T	S	S	J	A	R	R	A	E	J	J	Y	S
B	A	N	D	H	A	V	G	A	R	H	I	P	W	U
D	M	R	Z	U	Y	N	O	J	A	M	N	T	R	N
F	X	T	I	U	D	E	E	Q	G	C	T	A	F	D
H	E	N	E	S	D	H	Z	Y	N	H	V	W	K	A
T	M	Z	T	A	K	S	W	Y	A	E	W	C	N	R
M	S	Z	L	M	S	A	W	A	R	I	W	V	S	B
O	F	O	W	I	U	P	E	R	I	Y	A	R	K	A
C	E	S	E	Q	O	F	I	I	Z	G	P	Z	F	N
K	I	X	F	F	J	E	B	B	A	D	G	B	F	S
I	T	T	E	B	R	O	C	M	K	K	I	J	K	F
N	X	V	G	M	N	H	T	Z	P	O	R	Z	H	M
I	K	F	X	P	Q	Z	M	H	N	R	S	O	Y	X
O	X	E	Z	F	J	J	R	U	G	J	J	M	Z	W
G	V	T	L	V	S	E	B	S	K	C	K	P	C	Z

BANDHAVGARH

DUDHWA

GIR

CORBETT

KANHA

KAZIRANGA

KEOLADEO

PERIYAR

SARISKA

SUNDARBANS

15 **Measure the objects given below and write their size in centimetres, using the scale at the bottom of the page.**

.... cm

.... cm

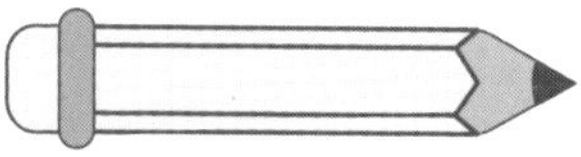

.... cm

.... cm

.... cm

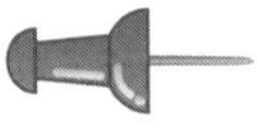

.... cm

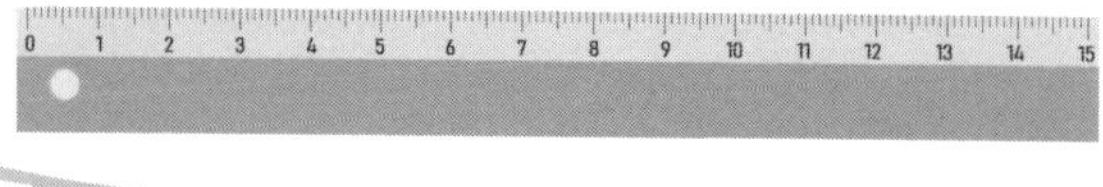

16 Match the shapes to make six perfect triangles.

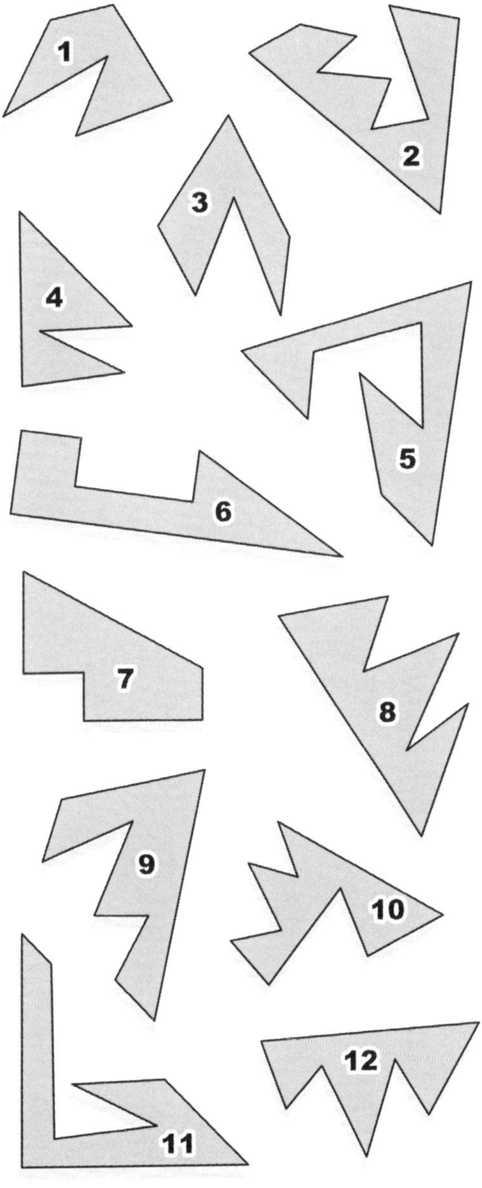

17 Match the fraction numbers with the image they represent.

18 Identify the mirror image of the picture in the box.

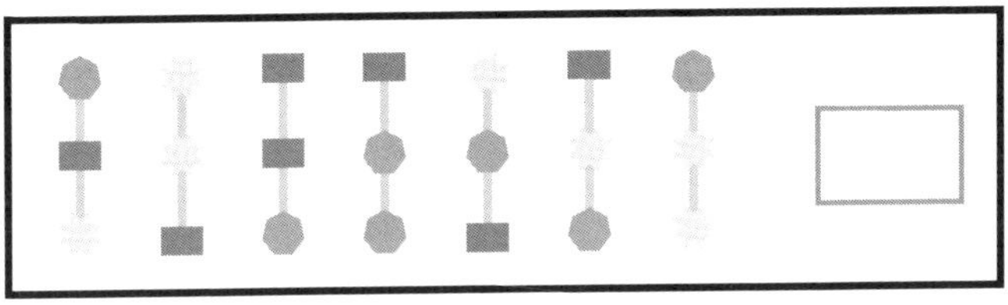

1. 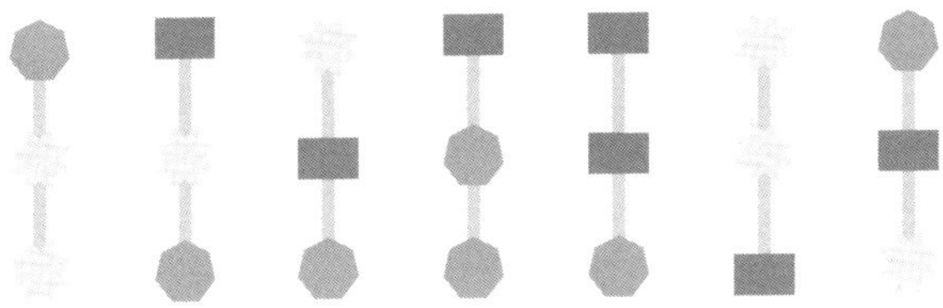

2. 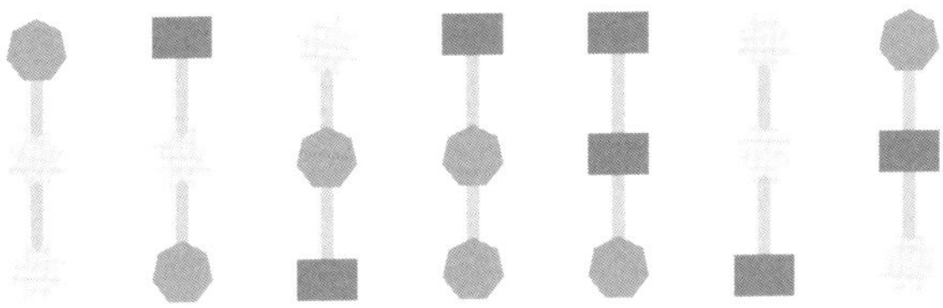

3. 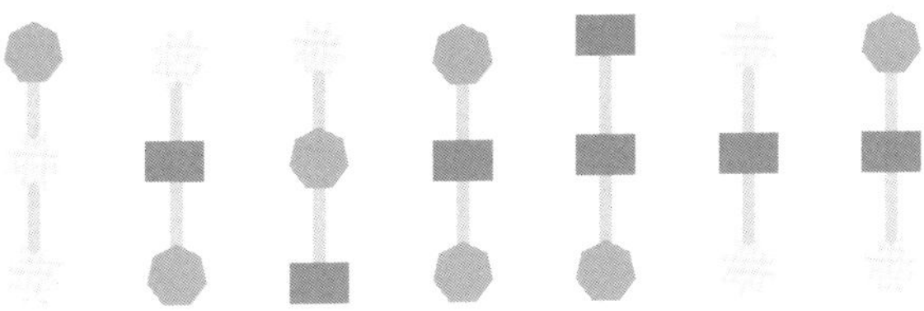

4. 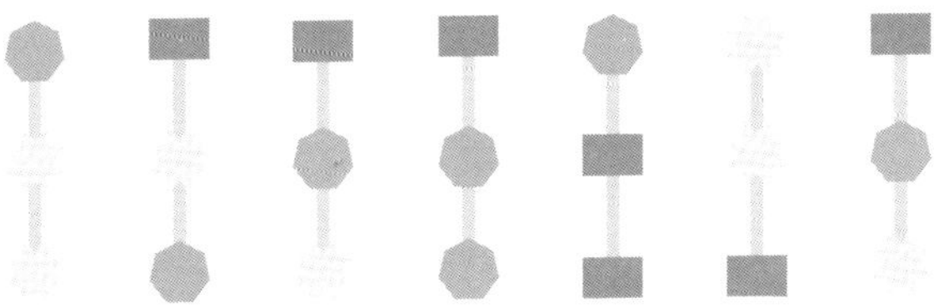

19 The carpenter's shop is a mess. Can you help him find objects that are of no use to him, in his workshop?

20 Can you help the robots find the correct sockets for charging themselves?

21 Solve the crossword with the clues given below.

Across

3. A series of Indian observation satellite

5. An experimental satellite built for the first flight of GSLV-D1

6. The world's lightest satellite

7. First satellite launched from an Indian launch vehicle.

10. India's first lunar probe

Down

1. India's first Mars orbiter

2. India's first multipurpose communication and weather satellite

4. First Indian Satellite

8. India's first experimental remote sensing satellite

9. The first meteorological satellite built by ISRO

22 Identify the logos of these social media platforms.

___________ ___________ ___________

___________ ___________ ___________

___________ ___________ ___________

23 Hidden in this word puzzle are the names of 10 Olympic medallists from India. Look for them vertically, horizontally and diagonally.

L	F	S	A	U	N	J	U	I	T	U	M	K	D	M
A	V	U	R	Z	H	W	A	M	V	M	Y	N	E	A
W	X	S	D	L	Q	D	X	W	D	H	A	C	H	R
H	J	H	N	G	E	I	I	W	N	H	H	F	W	Y
E	S	I	I	O	V	A	O	S	C	G	Z	U	Z	K
N	S	L	B	Z	G	N	N	N	V	S	E	Y	C	O
A	Z	K	V	I	U	Z	A	D	B	P	M	N	T	M
N	B	U	A	Z	T	Y	I	L	E	P	M	X	H	B
I	Y	M	N	L	H	I	V	F	D	R	A	I	J	T
A	G	A	I	D	I	H	C	I	B	M	P	G	U	R
S	K	R	H	G	A	G	A	N	N	A	R	A	N	G
M	T	C	B	D	Q	T	I	E	T	R	D	T	E	R
X	U	N	A	H	C	I	A	B	A	R	I	M	C	S
S	A	K	S	H	I	M	A	L	I	K	Z	N	V	A
M	X	O	C	K	V	M	G	J	R	C	N	O	F	B

ABHINAV BINDRA

DHYAN CHAND

GAGAN NARANG

LEANDER PAES

MARY KOM

MIRABAI CHANU

PV SIDHU

SAINA NEHWAL

SAKSHI MALIK

SUSHIL KUMAR

24 Help the kangaroo find the way to his home—Australia.

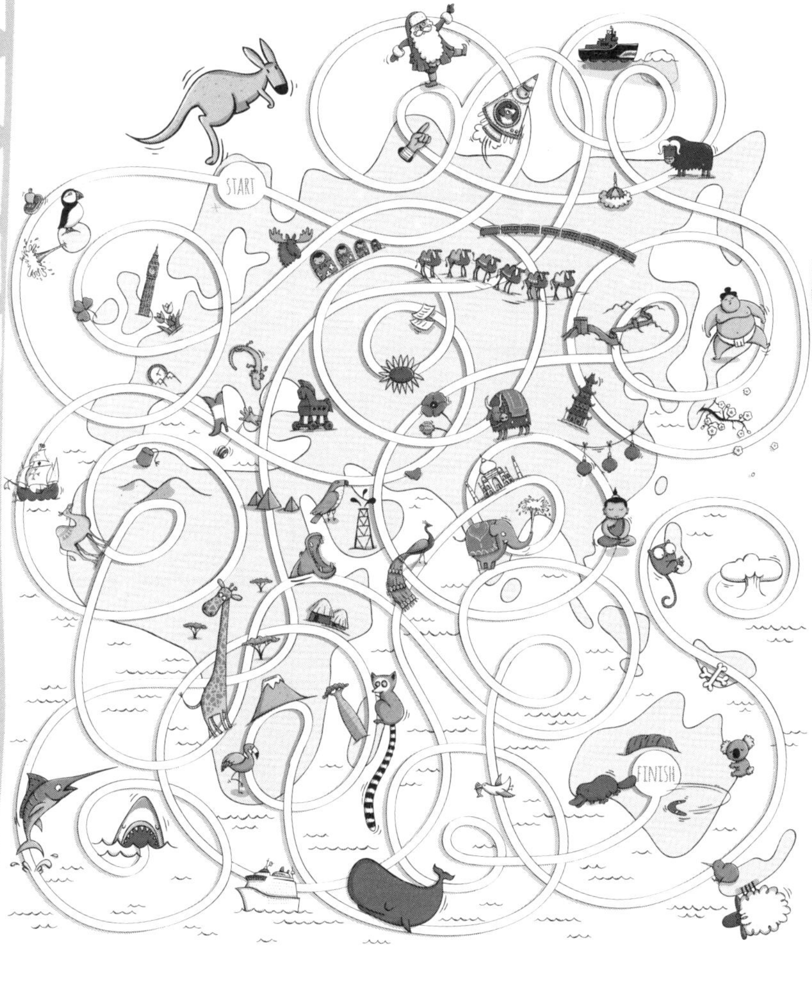

25 Solve the Sudoku. Arrange numbers 1-9 in each grid such that you don't repeat a number in a row, a column or a box.

<table>
<tr><td></td><td></td><td></td><td>7</td><td></td><td>2</td><td>5</td><td>9</td><td></td></tr>
<tr><td>2</td><td></td><td>8</td><td></td><td>3</td><td></td><td></td><td>4</td><td></td></tr>
<tr><td></td><td>5</td><td></td><td></td><td></td><td>9</td><td>8</td><td></td><td>2</td></tr>
<tr><td>1</td><td></td><td>2</td><td>3</td><td></td><td></td><td></td><td>7</td><td></td></tr>
<tr><td></td><td></td><td>5</td><td></td><td>2</td><td></td><td></td><td></td><td>1</td></tr>
<tr><td></td><td>8</td><td>3</td><td></td><td>6</td><td></td><td></td><td>5</td><td></td></tr>
<tr><td></td><td>1</td><td></td><td></td><td></td><td></td><td></td><td>2</td><td></td></tr>
<tr><td>5</td><td></td><td></td><td></td><td></td><td></td><td>9</td><td></td><td>3</td></tr>
<tr><td></td><td></td><td>4</td><td>9</td><td></td><td></td><td>6</td><td>1</td><td></td></tr>
</table>

26 Count the number of umbrellas, clouds, drops and snowflakes in the picture.

27 Can you identify these idioms?

1

2

3

4

5

6

28 Can you find your way through this maze of rooms with some open and some locked doors? Start from the top and avoid the closed doors.

29 Spot the odd one out.

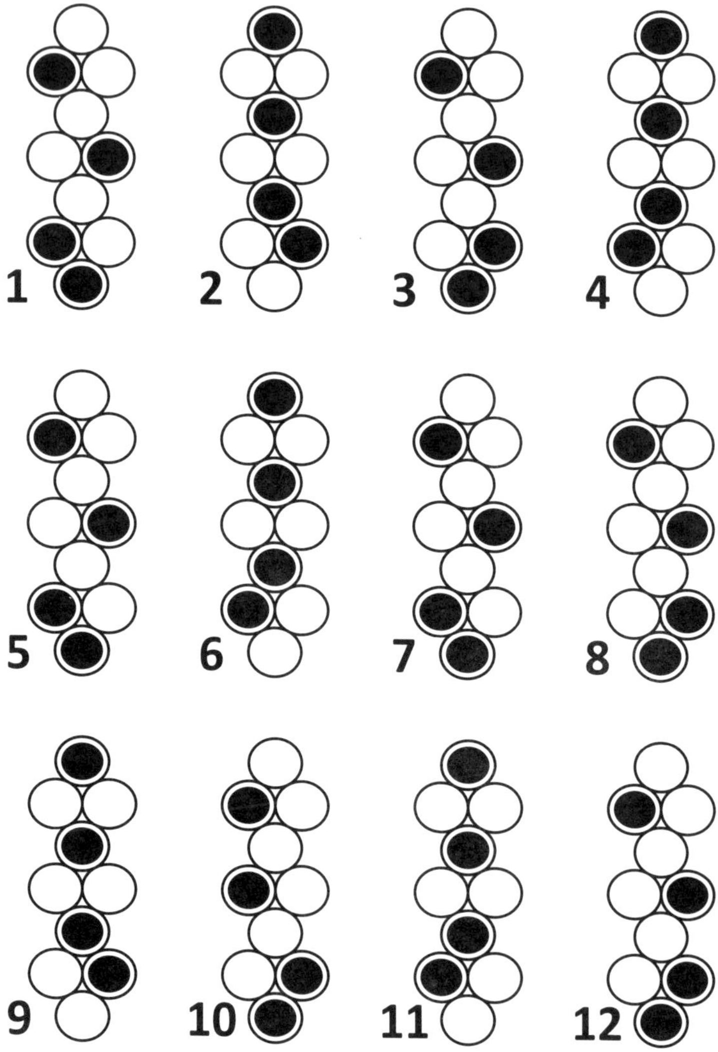

30 Re-arrange the letters to unscramble nine words associated with winter.

RESIK

FLOWKANSE

NIGTAKS

MOWNANS

STICNOAVA

STROF

DLOC

GELDSNIG

SECICLI

31 Gear 1 rotates clockwise; gears 5, 6 and 9 work together. Can you figure out the directions of gears 2, 3, 4, 7, 8 and 10?

hint When one gear rotates, the one that touches it rotates in the other direction. The gears with belts move in the same direction and crisscross ones move in the opposite direction.

32 Use your addition and subtraction skills to complete this fun maths puzzle.

8   5 + 2 = ___

−   −

___ − 5 = ___   6

=   +   +   =

1   ___ − 1 = ___

=   =

7 + ___ = ___

−

5 + ___ = ___

−   =

___ − 2 = ___

=

___ + 1 = 2

33 Hidden in this word puzzle are the names of some human body parts. You can find them vertically, horizontally and diagonally.

L	E	G	K	N	E	M	L	A	P
F	I	N	G	E	E	H	C	A	F
T	N	K	H	R	S	T	O	M	O
E	E	C	A	I	R	D	A	E	R
E	S	H	O	U	L	D	M	H	E
T	H	T	O	O	F	E	O	H	E
H	L	E	S	O	N	R	U	T	Y
E	I	P	E	Y	D	O	B	K	E
A	B	W	L	E	A	R	A	E	C
D	R	O	B	O	W	M	R	E	H

ARM
BODY
BROW
CHEEK
EAR
ELBOW

HEAD
KNEE
LEG
LIP
MOUTH
NECK

EYE
FINGER
FOOT
FOREHEAD
HAIR

NOSE
PALM
SHOULDER
STOMACH
TEETH

34 Find three unique cactuses.

35 Use logic to decipher the correct top view of the tower.

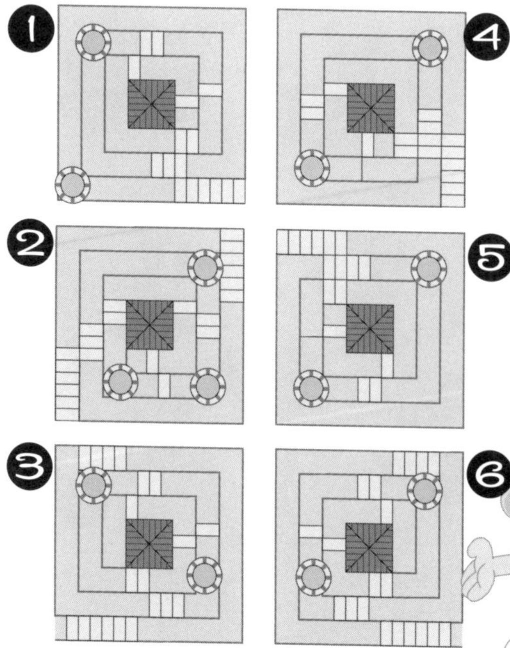

36 Match the questions with their correct answers.

1. What is a baby elephant called?
2. Patliputra was the ancient name of which city?
3. Name the organisation set up by Mother Teresa.
4. What did John Logie Baird invent?
5. Lala Lajpat Rai was also known as?

6. Who is the author of Panchatantra?
7. Which is the largest state in India, area-wise?
8. Which Indian city is called the City of Lakes?

9. What is the largest living animal in the world?
10. What is the folk dance of Gujarat known as?
11. Name the highest dam in India.

A. TEHRI DAM
B. PATNA
C. BLUE WHALE
D. UDAIPUR
E. RAJASTHAN
F. VISHNU SHARMA
G. PUNJAB KESARI
H. TELEVISION
I. MISSIONS OF CHARITY
J. GARBA
K. CALF

37 Identify the car brands from the logos given here.

38 Reposition just one matchstick in every row, to make a valid equation

V = III − II

IV − I = IV

VIII + I = XI

XI = X − I

X − V = X

XI − XX = IX

VII + V = I − I

39 Find the two identical keys.

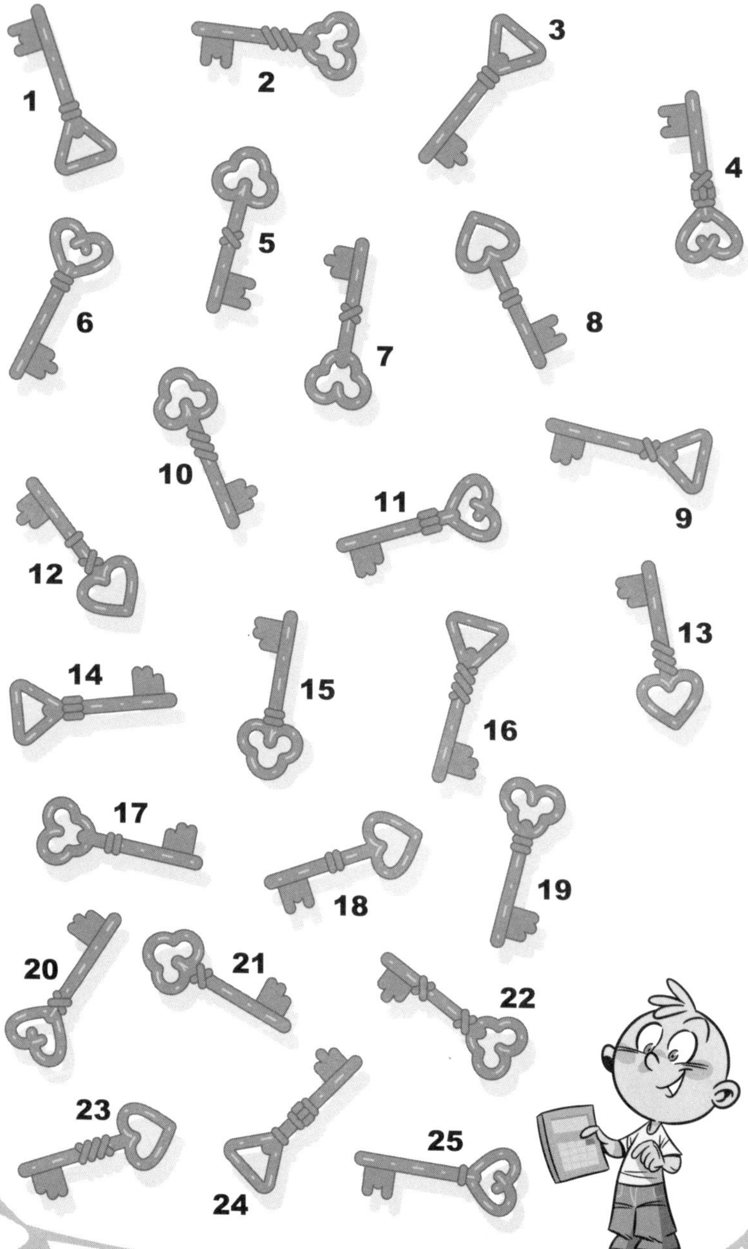

40 The first two hexagons in the box will combine to create a pretty pattern. Choose the correct pattern from the hexagons given below.

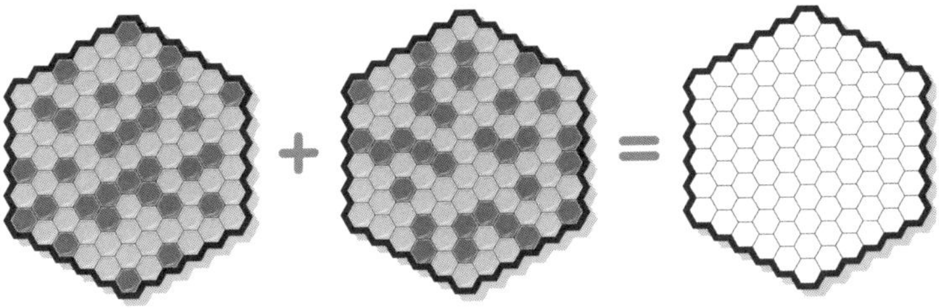

1

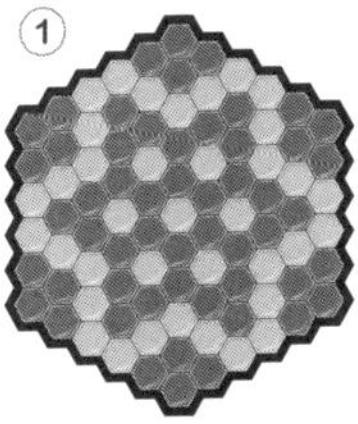

2

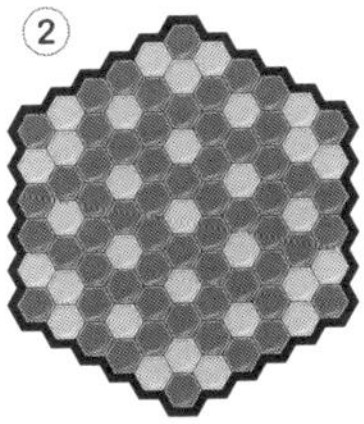

3

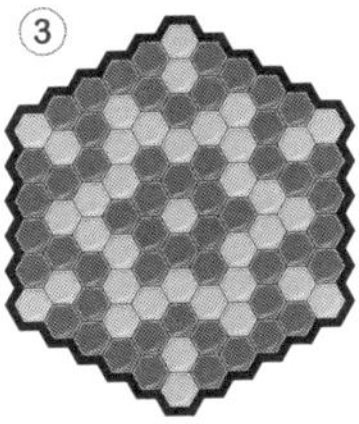

4

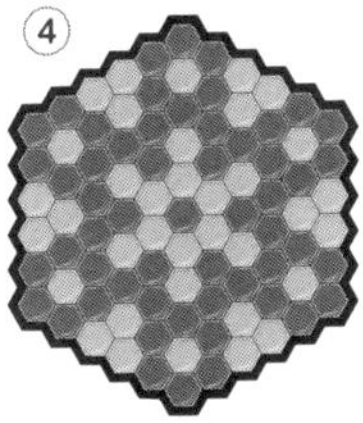

5

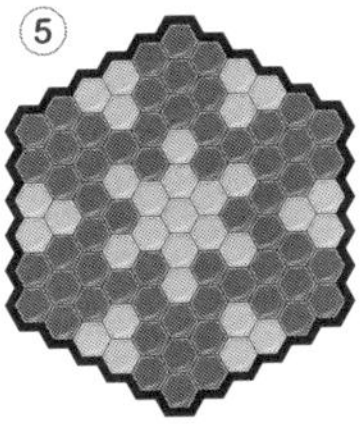

6

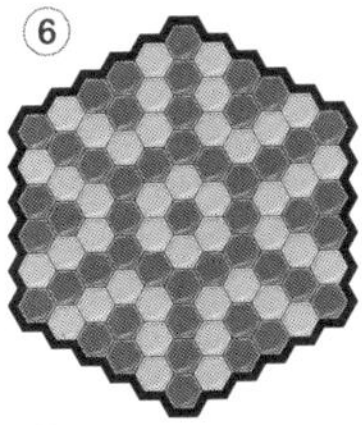

7

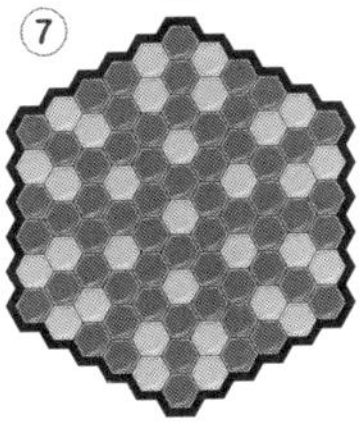

8

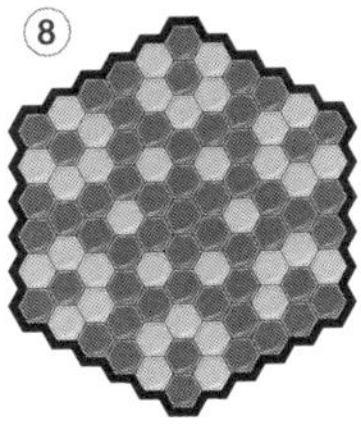

41

Find the hidden objects that are listed in the box, in the picture given below.

42 Untangle the phone wires and find out who the girl is calling.

43 How many shapes can you spot in the image below?

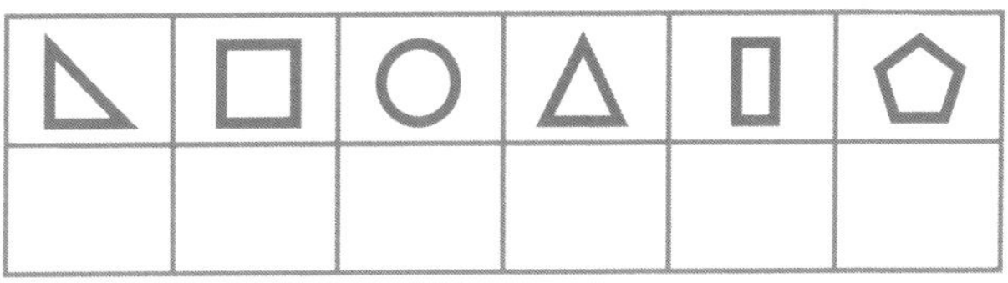

44 Use logic to fill in the missing numbers to complete this honeycomb Sudoku puzzle. Use numbers from 1 to 7 to fill up each horizontal and diagonal row, without repeating any number.

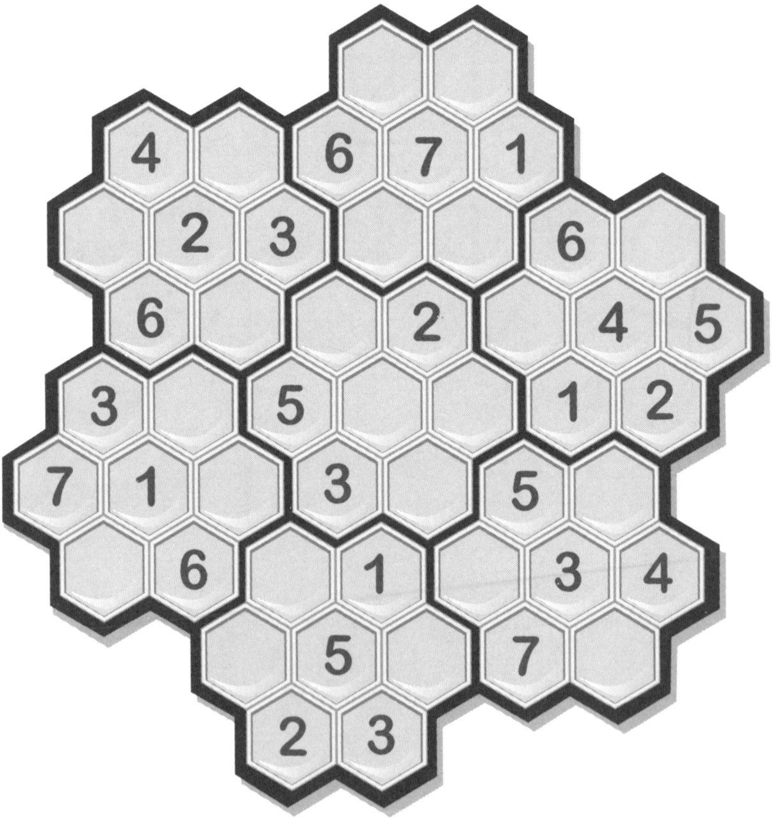

45 Separate the fruits and vegetables that grow above the ground and those that grow under the soil.

46 Arrange the blank spaces using the flowers in the top row. Each row and column should have all the highlighted flowers, without repetition.

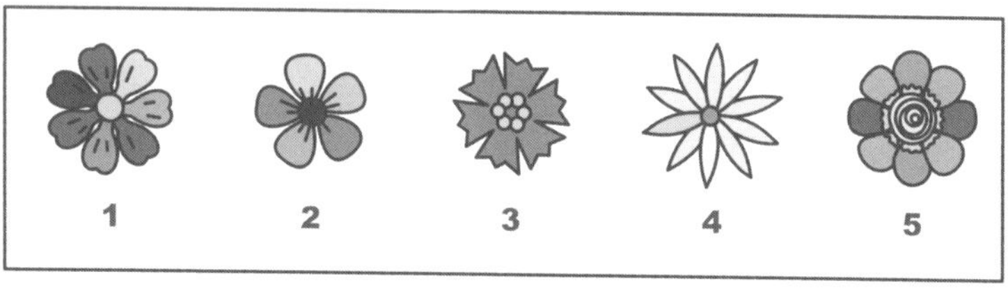

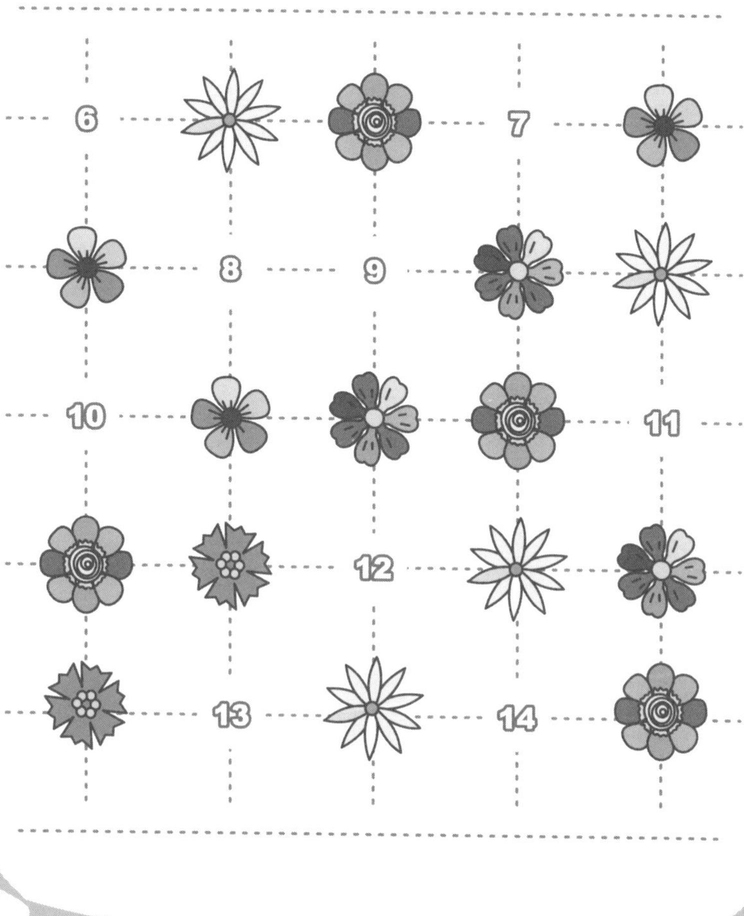

47 How many bats are there in this cave?

48 Solve the puzzle by drawing the dots and finding the correct places for all the remaining dominoes.

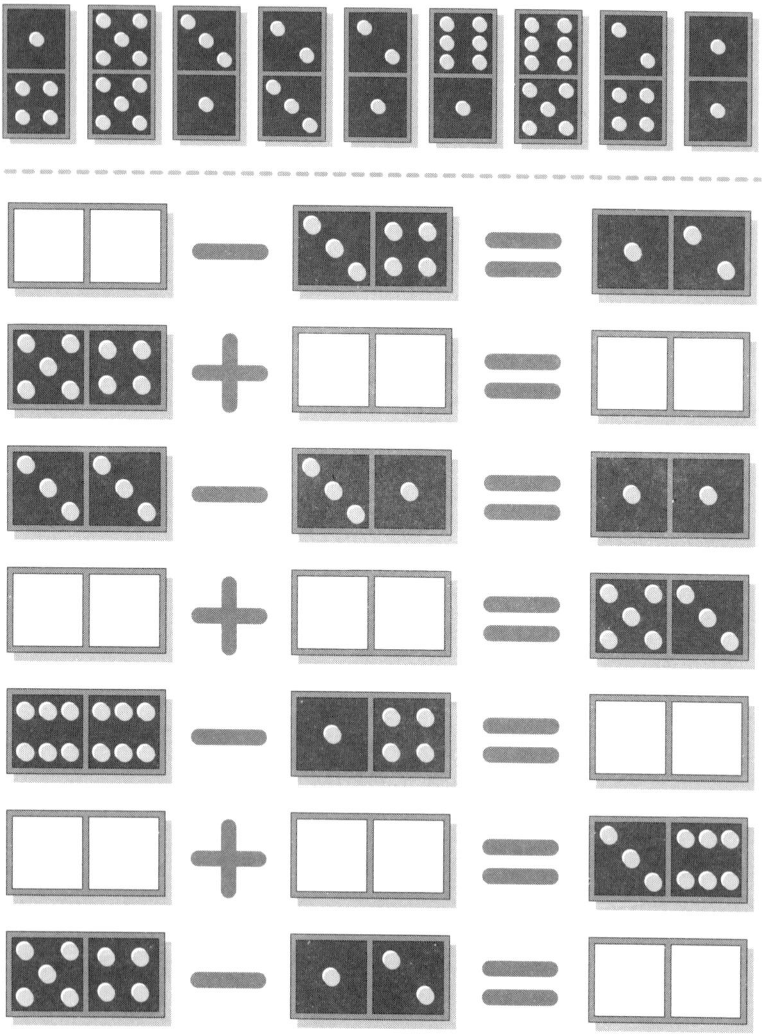

49 Use one big and one small snowflake to create new sequences, as given in the image. How many can you find?

50 Connect the scientists with their inventions and discoveries.

(B)

Anton Van Leeuwenhoek

(C)

Antoine Lavoisier

(D)

Dmitri Ivanovich Mendeleev

(E)

Thomas Edison

(A)

Louis Pasteur

1. Penicillin
2. Oxygen
3. Alternating current (AC) induction motor
4. Camera and projector
5. Food process called pasteurization
6. Bulb, gramophone, movie camera
7. Steam engine, copy machine
8. Periodic table of elements
9. First practical microscope
10. Telephone

(F)

James Watt

(G)

Alexander Fleming

(H)

Alexander Graham Bell

(I)

Nikola Tesla

(J)

Louis and Auguste Lumière

51 How much does each dessert cost?

52 Help the young cyclist find his way through the bicycle stadium to reach the finish line.

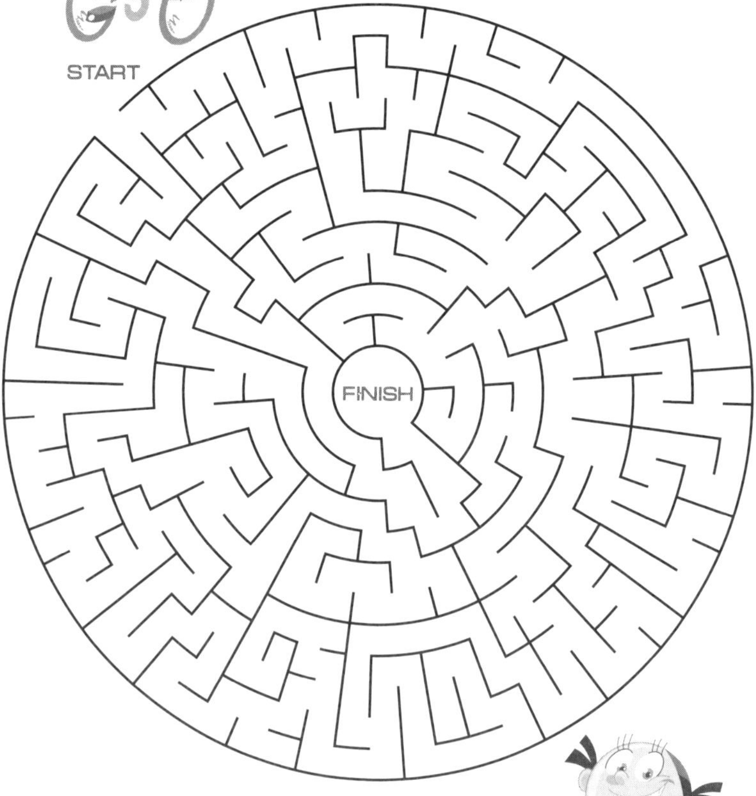

53 How many shapes can you spot in the image below?

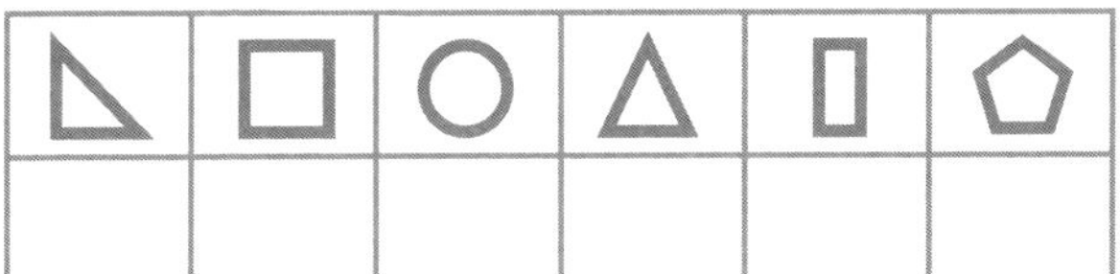

54 Help the archaeologists discover the room with the pharaoh's jewels. Beware of the mummies en route!

55 Guess the country from their flag.

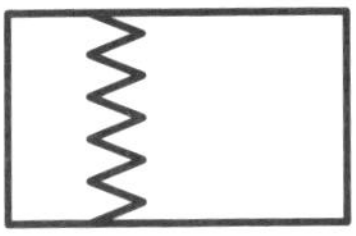

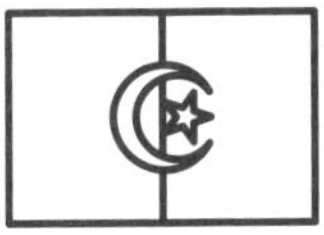

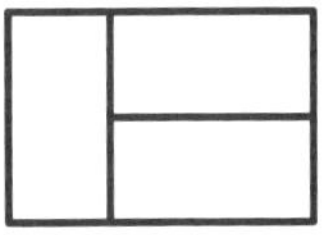

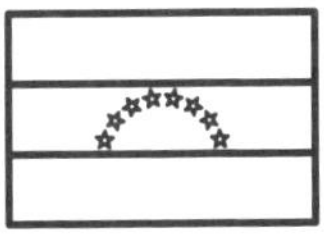

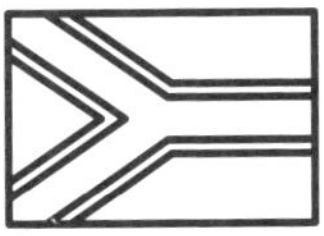

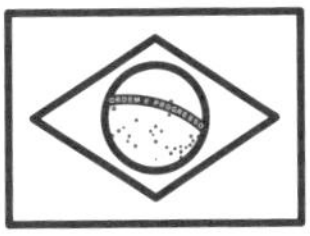

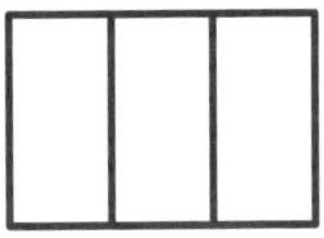

56 Vidya is a dancer. Her face is very expressive.

1. How many emotions does her face show?
2. How many faces show negative emotions, and how many display positive emotions?
3. How many faces are without head jewellery?
4. In how many images has Vidya shut her eyes?
5. How many faces have bindi on them?
6. How many faces show anger?

57 Which doorbell do the children need to ring to wake up their napping grandfather?

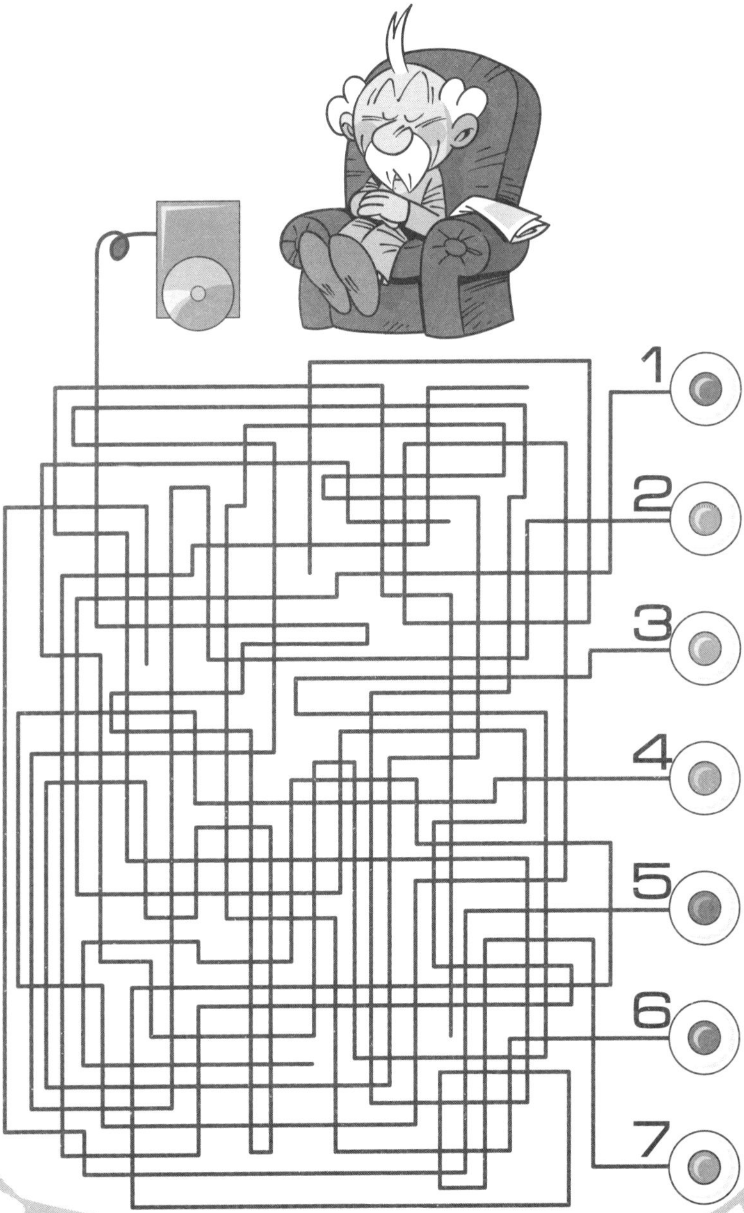

58 Gear number 1 rotates counter clockwise. Gears no. 5 and 10 are crossed-belt drives. What are the directions of gears 2, 3, 4, 6, 7, 8 and 9?

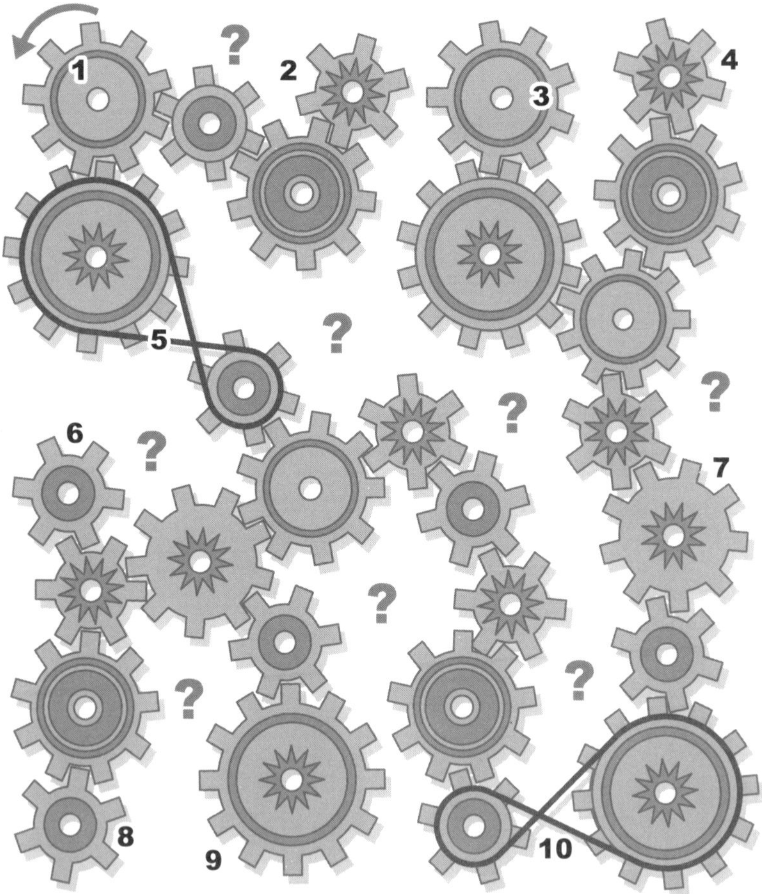

hint

When one gear rotates, the one that touches it rotates in the other direction. Gears with belts move in the same direction and the crisscross ones move in the opposite direction.

59 Search for the names of 10 Indian children's authors in the word puzzle. You can find them vertically, horizontally and diagonally.

L	N	R	U	Y	E	K	S	D	V	H	E	J	F	Q
A	O	A	P	D	G	M	A	N	F	J	E	F	E	B
L	C	W	T	O	P	N	V	O	V	U	E	Y	E	N
T	G	I	Y	A	P	I	I	B	M	K	H	T	E	A
I	Y	G	N	U	S	O	E	N	O	K	L	K	N	Y
J	O	Z	B	Z	N	H	K	I	J	S	O	R	T	A
N	R	U	A	W	C	C	A	K	K	N	K	R	D	N
A	A	P	A	Y	C	A	R	S	C	D	U	P	S	A
R	T	M	F	K	J	Q	N	U	I	M	I	O	I	N
Z	I	K	P	P	N	L	E	R	A	N	O	A	C	T
K	N	H	F	A	U	H	L	H	T	G	G	C	I	P
B	A	V	P	I	Y	Y	D	I	G	W	K	H	A	A
A	A	S	I	N	N	U	R	Y	H	K	W	R	B	I
K	G	S	K	Q	S	P	A	R	O	A	N	A	N	D
S	H	O	B	H	A	T	H	A	R	O	O	R	D	Z

ANANT PAI
ANITA ROY
KHYRUNNISA A.
NATASHA SINGH
PARO ANAND
RANJIT LAL
RUSKIN BOND
SAVIE KARNEL
SHOBHA THAROOR
SUDHA MURTY

60 Count the number of fish in the aquarium below.

61 Unscramble the words to find out the names of six endangered animals.

PARODEL

LEHAW

DANAP

CLABK MURLE

RAPOL EARB

RETIG

62 Help the worker repair the broken tools. Find the correct peg for all of them.

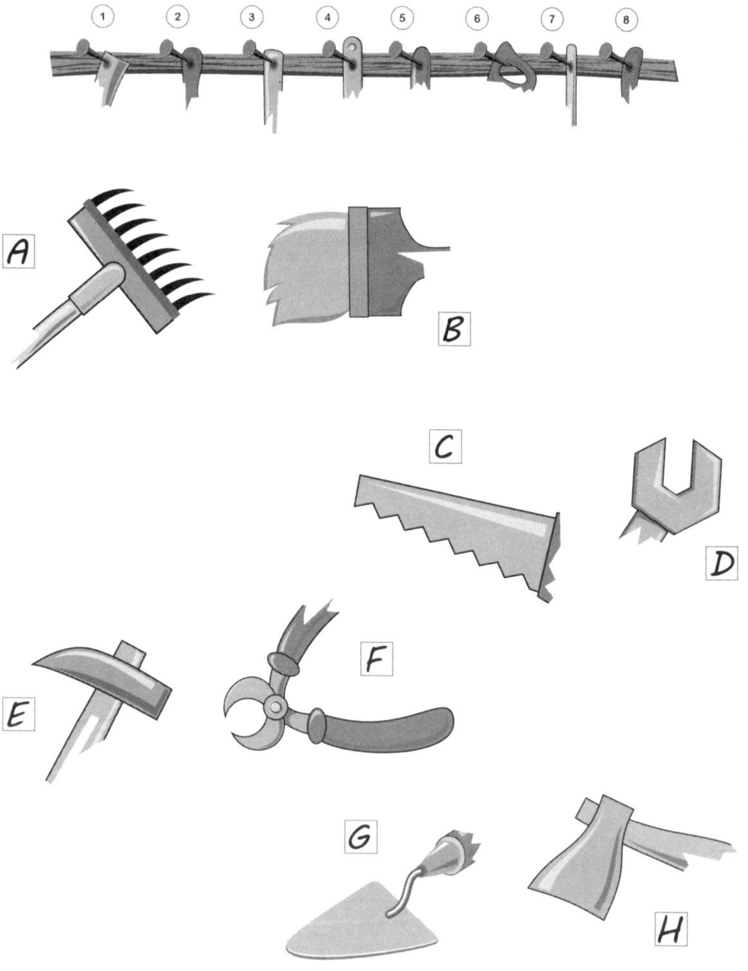

63 Can you guess the words and expressions in the rebus puzzles.

1

Please

2

WISH

★

3

Travel
―――
CCCCCC

4

MI1LLION

5

STOOD
―――
miss

6

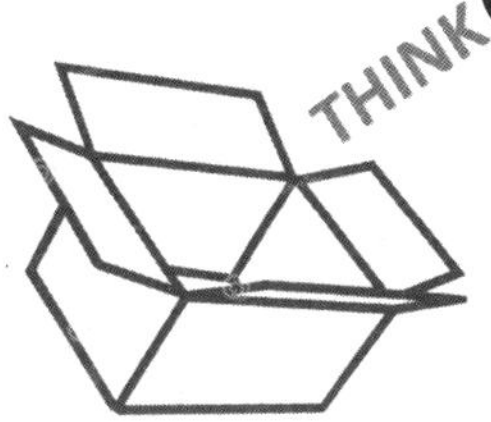

64 Complete the sequence by choosing the correct picture.

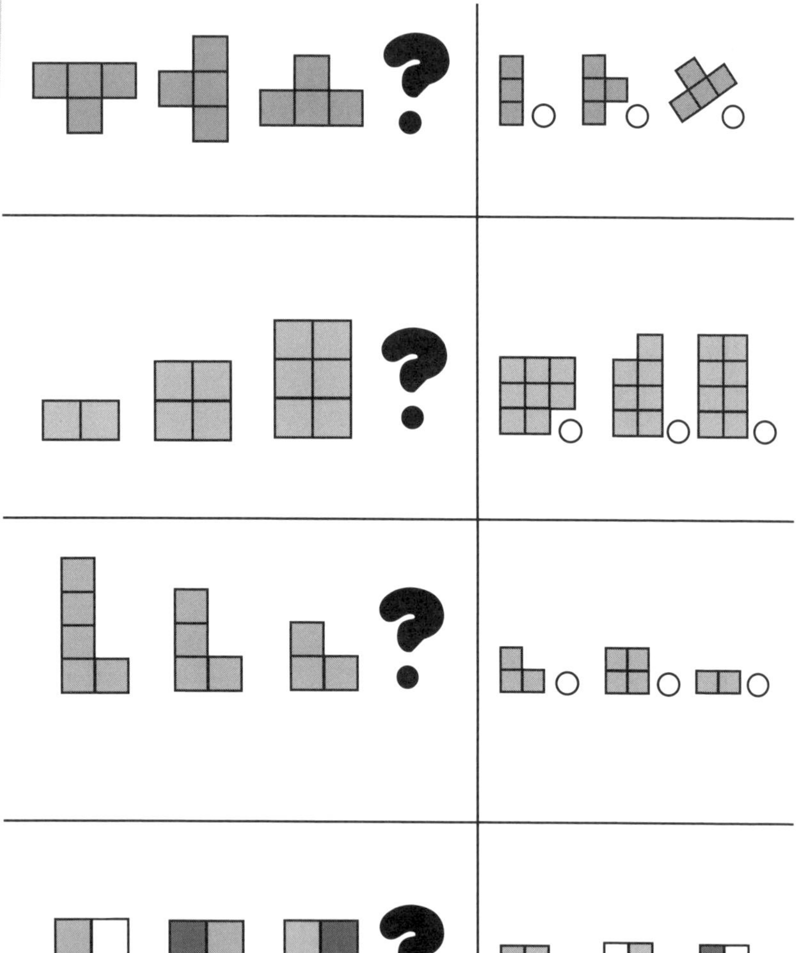

65 Unscramble the words to find the names of a few Indian monuments.

1. TRUAHPFE IIRKS

2. TONMU YARM

3. TJNARA ATNRAM

4. ARKOKN MTLEPE

5. HSNCAI UTSAP

6. RAHRAIMNC

7. JSNARULAG SUMUEM

8. RVYTOCI RWEOT

9. WAAH HAMLA

10. TVOIRCTA IRMLMEOA

66 Find the missing piece of the puzzle to figure out the correct phone number.

02334516
02759246
02953816
02827576
02905046
02907316
02927546
02426546
02121546

67 Find the two identical clocks.

68

Here is a tough one! Find at least 10 differences between the two images.

12

69 Unscramble the name and guess the animal.

RTULTE

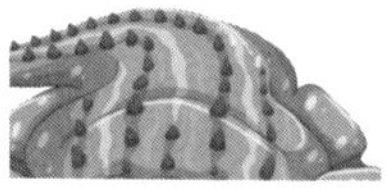

ROCOCILED

OHPIP

CARONO

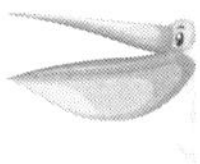

CPLIAEN

NIROH

70 Connect the currency with the country.

$ Dollar

¥ Yuan

ريال Riyal

₱ Peso

₩ Won

R$ Real

₪ Shekel

C$ Dollar

China	Cuba	Brazil	Israel
Saudi Arabia	Korea	Canada	US

71 Draw lines between the honeycombs to create segments of five cells each. Each segment should have five different insects.

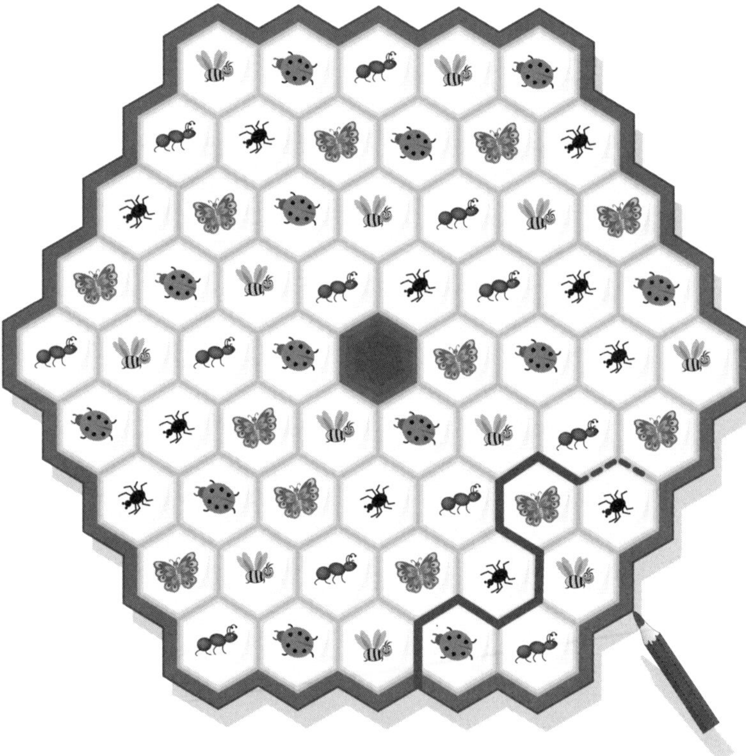

72 Find the two identical aeroplanes.

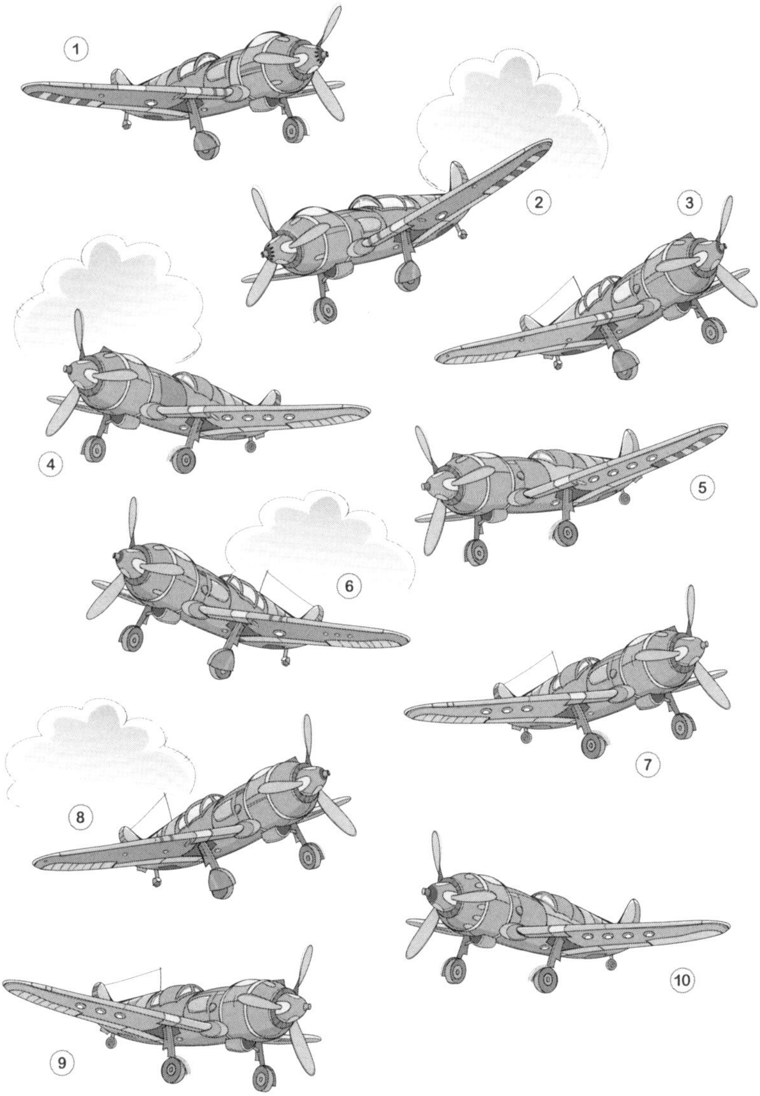

73 Guess the animals by their silhouettes.

74 Find the two identical ghosts.

75 Follow the directions given by the arrows in the picture clues below. If the 'Start' cell is your beginning point, find out which picture will each set of directions take you to.

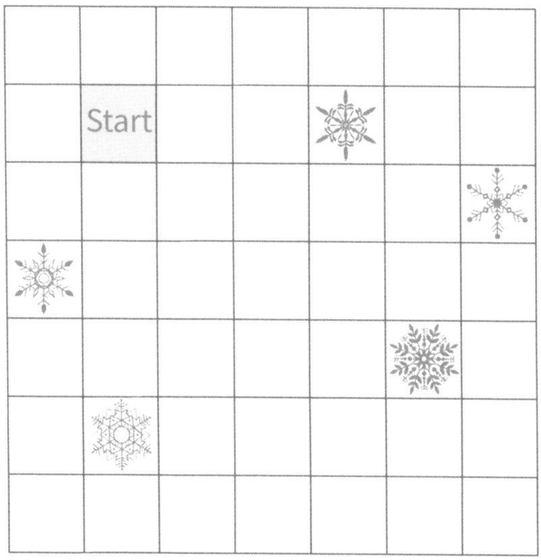

1. ↓ ↓ → ↓ → ↑ → ↓ →
2. ← ↓ → ↓ → → ↓ ← ↓ ←
3. ↑ → ↓ ↓ → ↓ → ↑ ↑
4. → ↓ ↓ → ↓ → ↑ ↑ → →
5. ↑ → ↓ → ↓ ↓ ← ↓ ← ← ↑

76 Find the hidden objects: 16 animals, 6 balloons, 5 hearts, a Christmas tree, an egg and a bone.

77 Match the figures with their cluster of shapes.

78 Search for the names of 10 Indian sweets in the word puzzle. You can find them vertically, horizontally and diagonally.

W F L T E V A W E V Q T B P I
D Y G I H V H L J H O K M A B
S K A A N O R H L Q T O Q Y E
M Y S O R E P A K U D I Q A L
R G A R E E H S L A G I P S A
A P U A C S G W K F Y S U A J
V S O L E J T F F L H V A M I
E N J D A D Q O T Z M O O R P
H U N I Z B W Z X F Y W T W N
G A I G A K J O J K W Y E G X
S Y U N D V I A O H W Y Q M U
M C Y Z N U E X M E G P X K C
F V O A W D O B E U F J F K E
U D B J M I B X O R N M X S R
J O P Z R Q H W V Y H M T H O

RASGULLA
JALEBI
SANDESH
MYSORE PAK
GULAB JAMUN
PAYASAM
MODAK
SHEERA
PITHE
GHEVAR

79 Help the dog reach the bone.

80 Can you guess the words and expressions in the rebus puzzles.

1

arrest
———
YOU ARE

2

FA ST

3

SECRET (circled)
SECRET
SECRET

4

Hill

5

NOBODY
———
LAW

6

GEGS
SGGE
ESGG
SGEG

81 How much does a car cost?

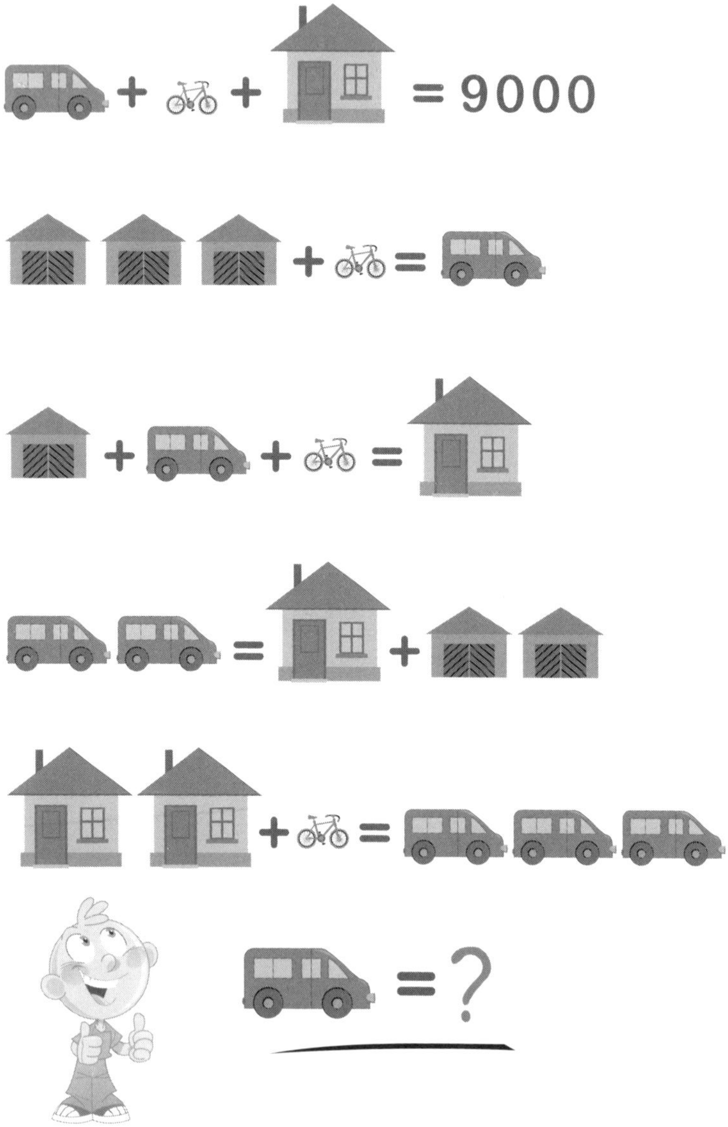

82 Add numbers to complete the equations.

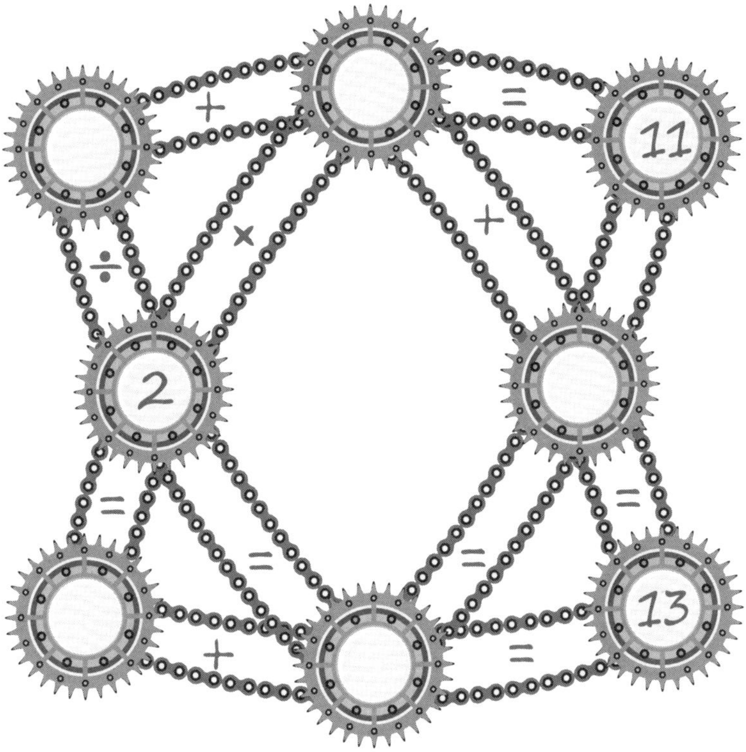

83 Help the worker finish building the houses. Find the missing part for each building.

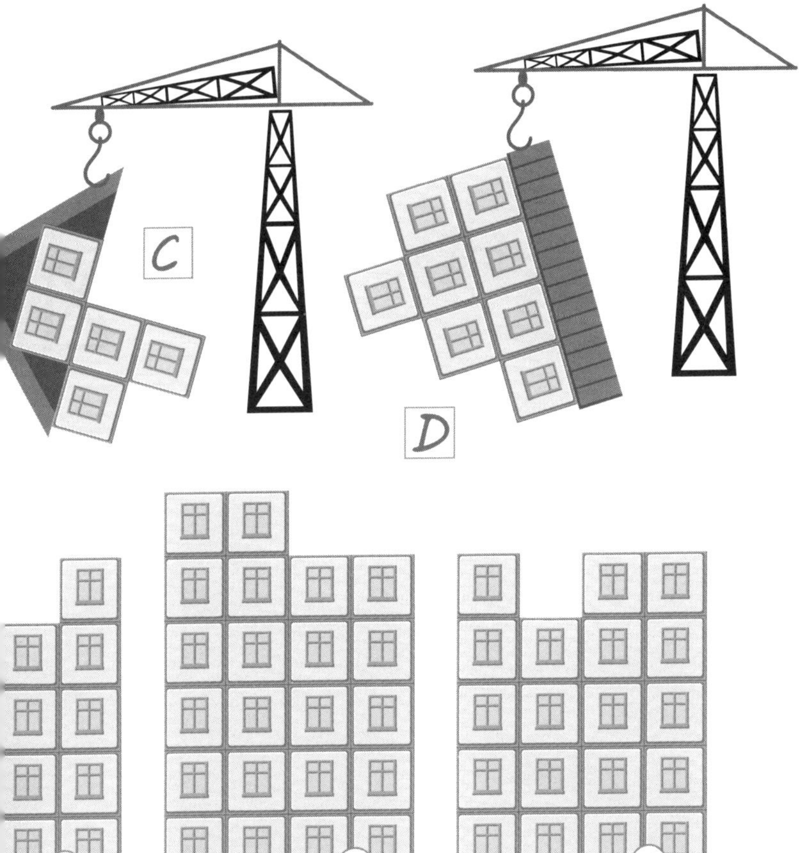
C
D
2
3
4

84 Move two matchsticks to make seven squares.

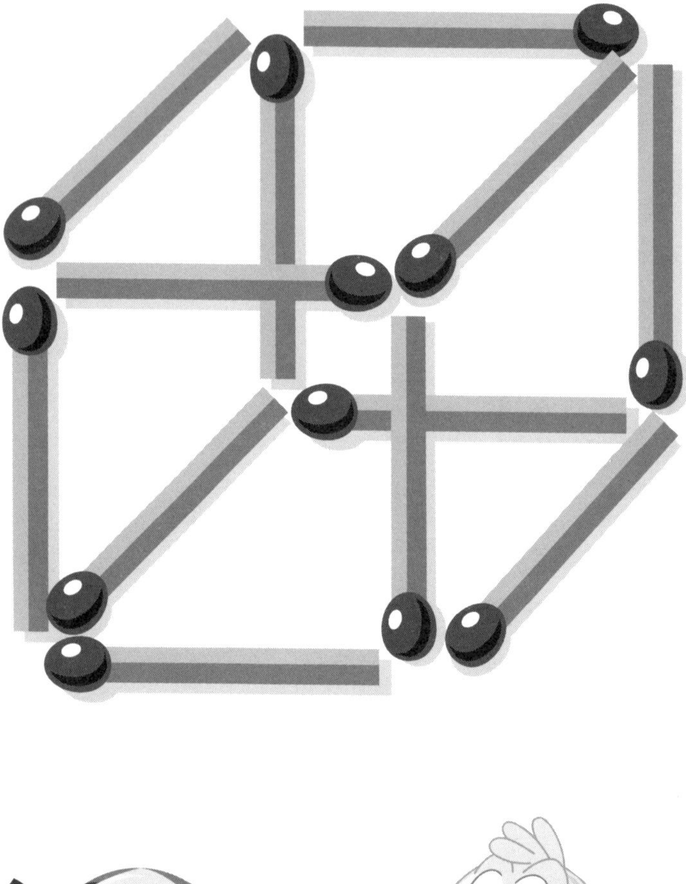

85 Take a look at the pictures and guess the idiom.

1

2

3

4

5

6

86 Find the two identical dice.

87 How much does each fruit cost?

88 How many trees does this forest have? Can you count the different varieties of trees?

89 Solve the Sudoku. Arrange numbers 1-9 in each grid of nine numbers such that you don't repeat a number. A number shouldn't be used twice in a row or a column.

8		2		1	3	5		
	9			5			3	1
5			9	8		6	7	
9		6			8			5
	4		5		1	9		
1				2			6	3
4		9			2	1		
	8		7	4			9	6
	3		1		6	2		

90 How much do you know about India's freedom struggle? Read the statements and mark them as true or false.

1. Bhagat Singh, Sukhdev Rajguru and Jai Gopal were involved in the Lahore conspiracy case to avenge the killing of Lal Lajpat Rai. ☐

2. The Indian National Congress declared Purna Swaraj at the Congress session at Karachi, in 1930. ☐

3. Mehsana in Gujarat is known for Mahatma Gandhi's famous Salt March. ☐

4. The first Prime Minister Jawaharlal Nehru raised the Indian National Flag on 15 August, 1947 at the Red Fort. ☐

5. Netaji Subhash Chandra Bose is credited for giving the nation the slogan 'Inquilab Zindabad'. ☐

6

Freedom fighter Chandra Shekhar Azad famously said 'Give me blood and I will give you freedom'.

7

The first non-co-operation movement was started in India by the freedom fighter Mangal Pandey in 1857.

8

Jawahar Lal Nehru started The Independent at Allahabad, in 1919.

9

Dadabhai Naoroji was said to be the Father and Founder of The Indian National Congress.

10

The poet Rabindranath Tagore composed 'Jana Gana Mana,' the National Anthem of India.

91 How many words can you make from the letters in the word MANIFEST?

7 letter words

6 letter words

5 letter words

4 letter words

92 Buried in this pile of toys are the kids' favourite toys. Can you help them find the toys and spot 10 hidden cats while you are at it?

93 Find B in 30 seconds!

RRRRRRRRRRRRRRRRRRRRRRRRRRRRRRRRRR
RRRRRRRRRRRRRRRRRRRRRRRRRRRRRRRRRR
RRRRRRRRRRRRRRRRRRRRRRRRRRRRRRRRRR
RRRRRRRRRRRRRRRRRRRRRRRRRRRRRRRRRR
RRRRRRRRRRRRRRRRRRRRRRRRRRRRRRRRRR
RRRRRRRRRRRRRRRRRRRRRRRRRRRRRRRRRR
RRRRRRRRRRRRRRRRRRRRRRRRRRRRRRRRRR
RRRRRRRRRRRRRRRRRRRRRRRRRRRRRRRRRR
RRRRRRRRRRRRRRRRRRRRRRRRRRRRRRRRRR
RRRRRRRRRRRRRRRRRRRRRRRRRRRRRRRRRR
RRRRRRRRRRRRRRRRRRRRRRRRRRRRRRRRRR
RRRRRRRRRRRRRRRRRRRRRRRRRRRRRRRRRR
RRRRRRRRRRRRRRRRRRRRRRRRRRRRRRRRRR
RRRRRRRRRRRRRRRRRRRRRRRRRRRRRRRRRR
RRRRRRRRRRRRRRRRRRRRRRRRBRRRRRRRRR
RRRRRRRRRRRRRRRRRRRRRRRRRRRRRRRRRR
RRRRRRRRRRRRRRRRRRRRRRRRRRRRRRRRRR
RRRRRRRRRRRRRRRRRRRRRRRRRRRRRRRRRR
RRRRRRRRRRRRRRRRRRRRRRRRRRRRRRRRRR
RRRRRRRRRRRRRRRRRRRRRRRRRRRRRRRRRR
RRRRRRRRRRRRRRRRRRRRRRRRRRRRRRRRRR
RRRRRRRRRRRRRRRRRRRRRRRRRRRRRRRRRR
RRRRRRRRRRRRRRRRRRRRRRRRBRRRRRRRRR
RRRRRRRRRRRRRRRRRRRRRRRRRRRRRRRRRR
RRRRRRRRRRRRRRRRRRRRRRRRRRRRRRRRRR
RRRRRRRRRRRRRRRRRRRRRRRRRRRRRRRRRR
RRRRRRRRRRRRRRRRRRRRRRRRRRRRRRRRRR
RRRRRRRRRRRRRRRRRRRRRRRRRRRRRRRRRR
RRRRRRRRRRRRRRRRRRRRRRRRRRRRRRRRRR
RRRRRRRRRRRRRRRRRRRRRRRRRRRRRRRRRR
RRRRRRRRRRRRRRRRRRRRRRRRRRRRRRRRRR
RRRRRRRRRRRRRRRRRRRRRRRRRRRRRRRRRR
RRRRRRRRRRRRRRRRRRRRRRRRRRRRRRRRRR
RRRRRRRRRRRRRRRRRRRRRRRRRRRRRRRRRR
RRRRRRRRRRRRRRRRRRRRRRRRRRRRRRRRRR

94 What comes next ...?

1	3	5	7	9	?
1	2	4	8	16	?
1	2	3	5	8	?
9	7	5	3	?	
8	4	2	1	?	
12	15	18	111	?	

95 Search for 10 words and their anagrams provided in the box below. You can find them vertically, horizontally or diagonally.

X	J	P	D	I	A	R	C	B	X	E	A	S	X	H	J	Z	J
Y	T	H	U	J	L	K	Y	E	K	B	E	E	V	T	C	I	W
H	C	F	S	D	Q	U	N	L	H	S	D	C	H	E	A	P	B
C	R	I	T	P	R	O	G	O	L	C	W	B	R	H	R	T	O
I	I	W	Y	V	A	V	O	W	U	W	M	G	J	O	J	K	R
D	C	P	C	B	I	R	Q	N	I	G	H	T	H	U	B	F	E
E	R	T	E	H	R	N	S	H	I	R	E	O	Z	S	A	E	D
R	I	H	V	A	I	A	C	L	Z	M	L	G	C	T	K	L	D
G	E	I	Y	T	C	N	G	H	E	F	B	A	Z	U	A	F	W
O	D	N	I	S	L	H	W	Z	W	Y	O	P	G	D	P	O	H
T	X	G	G	R	A	B	U	U	P	H	W	O	Z	Y	G	O	Y
C	F	Z	J	Z	R	A	P	L	A	Y	E	R	S	M	U	J	F

ARC
BELOW
BORED
BRAG
CAR
CHEAP
CHIN

CIDER
CRIED
DUSTY
ELBOW
GRAB
INCH
NIGHT

PARSLEY
PEACH
PLAYERS
ROBED
STUDY
THING

96 Look at the silhouettes of these baseball players carefully and answer the following questions.

1 How many players have a bat in their hands?

2 How many are pitching?

3 How many are fielding or catching the ball?

4 How many players are wearing a headgear?

97 Can you guess the words and expressions in the rebus puzzles.

1

PROMISE

2

+ VERB

3

eCONOMY

4

JACK

5

S
T
A ME
N
D

6

BE

98 Identify the currencies given below.

₿	€	£
₨	₹	ريال
TL	¥	฿
A$	C$	Fr

99 Find the objects in the box given below.

100 How many Ms can you find in 30 seconds?

WWWWWWWWWWWWWWWWWWWWWW
WWWWWWWWWWWWWWWWWWWWWW
WWWWWWWWWWWWWWWWWWWWWM
WWWWWWWWWWWWWWWWWWWWWW
WWWWWWWWWWWWWWWWWWWWWW
WWWWWMWWWWWWWWWWWWWWWW
WWWWWWWWWWWWWWWWWWWWWW
WWWWWWWWWWWWWWWWWWWWWW
WWWWWWWWWWWWWWWWWWWWWW
WWWWWWWWWWWWWWWWWWWWWW
WWWWWWWWWWWWWWWWWWWWWW
WWWWWWWWWWWWWWWWWWWWWW
WWWWWWWWWWWWWWWWWWWWWW
WWWWWWWWWWWWWWWWWWWWWW
WWWWWWWWWWWMWWWWWWWWWW
WWWWWWWWWWWWWWWWWWWWWW
WWWWWWWWWWWWWWWWWWWWWW
WWWWWWWWWWWWWWWWWWWWWW
WWWWWWWWWWWWWWWWWWWWWW
WWWWWWWWWWWWWWWWWWWWWW
WWWWMWWWWWWWWWWWWWWWWW
WWWWWWWWWWWWWWWWWWWWWW
WWWWWWWWWWWWWWWWWWWWWW
WWWWWWWWWWWWWWWWWWWWWW
WWWWWWWWWWWWWWWWWWWWWW
WWWWWWWWWWWWWWWWWMWWWW
WWWWWWWWWWWWWWWWWWWWWW
WWWWWWWWWWWWWWWWWWWWWW
WWWWWWWWWWWWWWWWWWWWWW

101 One artefact in the stack is missing from the shelf. Can you find it?

102 Identify the sport from the balls given below.

______ ______ ______

______ ______ ______

______ ______ ______

______

103 Find all the number from 1 to 100 successively. Which number is missing?

17 61 23 33 80 50 54
14 25 69 51 43
4 24 39 58 28 95 63
70 98 59
32 46 57 35 42 52
44 49 5 48 53 62 41 1
47 79 13 93 71
64 68 92 27 75
15 45 6
81 55 9 40 78 31 66
74 99 73 100 91 34 3 60 18
38 85 12 29 76 19 56
82 37 26 20
72 16 88 87 22 77 2 89 30
86 96 94 84 7 97 90
36 65 21 11 8 67 10

104 Guess the countries from the given clues.

1. Gift of Nile
   E_ _ _ _
2. Holy Land
   P_ _ _ _ T_ _ _
3. Land of Maple
   C _ _ _ _ _
4. Land of Midnight Sun
   N_ _ _ _ _
5. Land of Rising Sun
   J_ _ _ _
6. Land of White Elephant
   T_ _ _ _ _ _ _
7. Play Ground of Europe
   S_ _ _ _ _ _ _ _ _ _
8. Sugar Bowl of the world
   C_ _ _

105 Unscramble the names of the Indian dance forms.

ALKBIAEYL

OMINITYATAMH

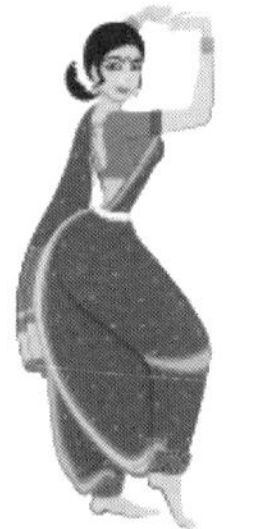

IVALAN

IPMNAURI

KTKHAA

MHOOGRA

AYATNMBAHAART

UCDUHNHI

106 Figure out the value of each card and write them in the circle.

♠ × ♥ = ♣

♣ + ♠ = ♦ + ♦

♦ + ♠ = ♣ − ♦

♥ × ♦ = ♣ + ♣ + ♣

♣ + ♦ + ♠ + ♥ = 23

♠ = ◯ ♥ = ◯ ♦ = ◯ ♣ = ◯

107 Figure out the value of each magic symbol and help the little girl count the value of the numbers.

108 Find the correct reflection for each set of playing cards.

109 Match the equipment with the sport.

1. Rowing
2. Table Tennis
3. Athletics
4. Football
5. Boxing
6. Badminton
7. Swimming
8. Baseball
9. Volleyball
10. Weightlifting
11. Skipping
12. Yoga
13. Ice skating
14. Polo

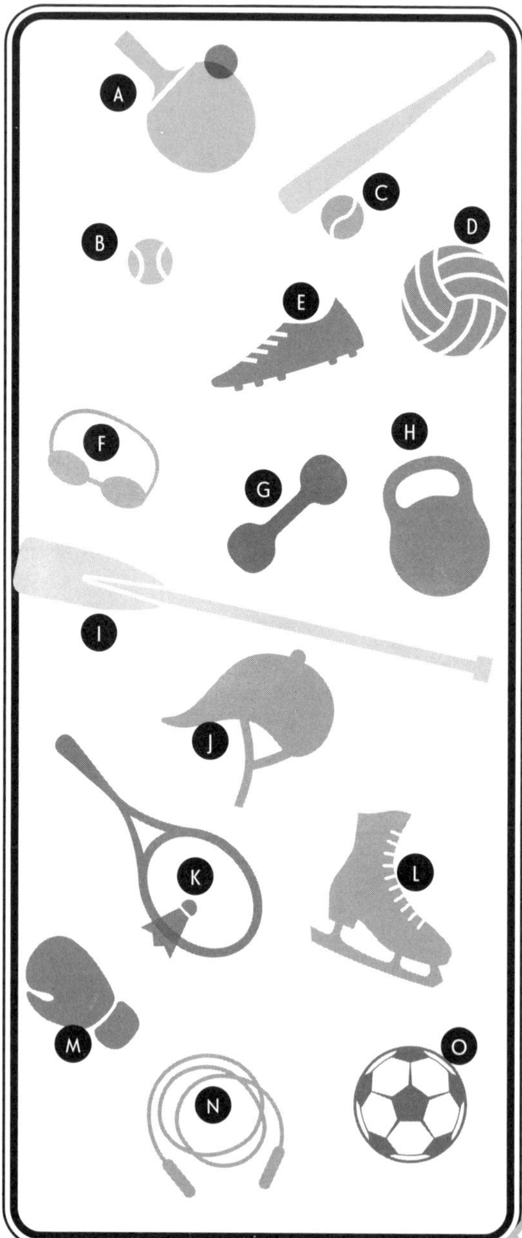

110 Match the shapes to make seven circles.

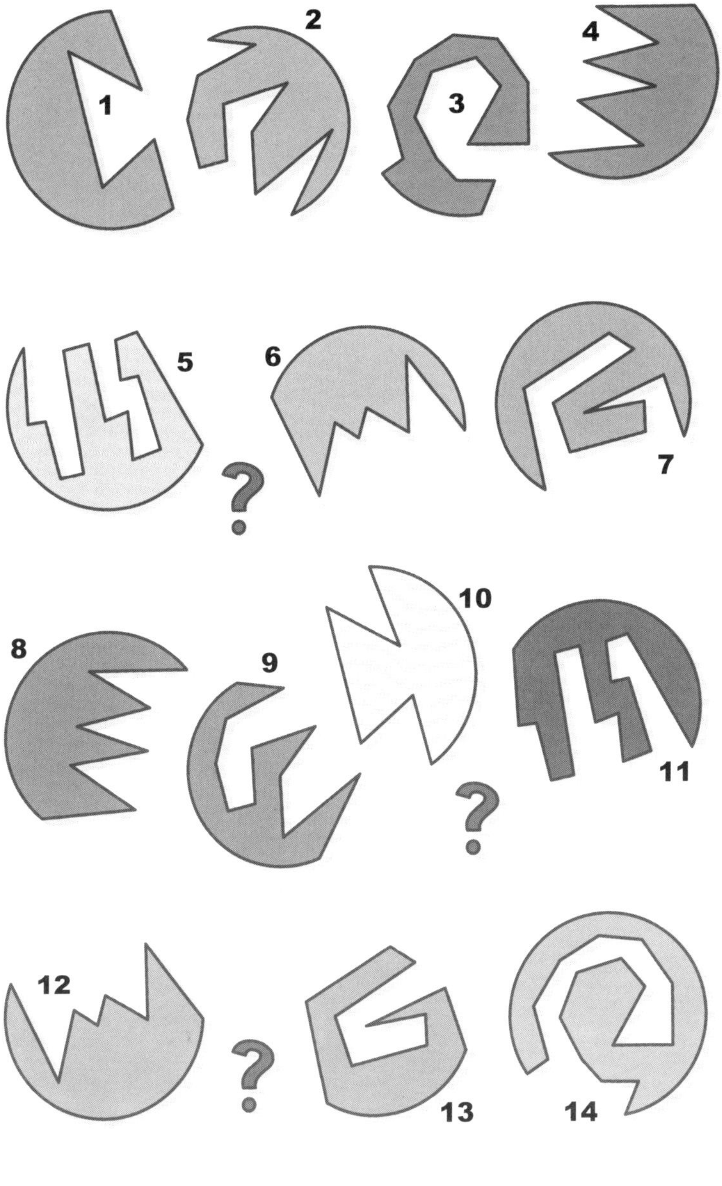

Answers

1. 18

2. d.

3. 

4. A. 8, B. 4, C. 3, D. 2, E. 5, F. 16, G. 7, H. 15

5.
   1. Couch potato
   2. Hold your horses
   3. Finding a needle in a haystack
   4. Digging your grave
   5. In a nutshell
   6. A bull in a China shop

6. 

7. 

8. Organic | Glass | Metal
Plastic | Paper | E-Waste

9. 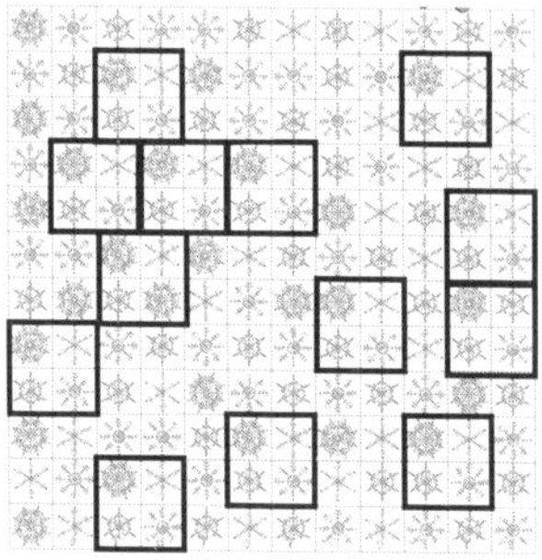

10.

11 + 1 = 12	10 + 2 = 12	4 + 8 = 12	6 + 6 = 12	11 + 3 = 14	
9 + 9 = 18	17 + 2 = 19			13 + 3 = 16	2 + 6 = 8
3 + 5 = 8	6 + 2 = 8	15 + 4 = 19	7 + 3 = 10	7 + 1 = 8	17 + 1 = 18
18 + 1 = 19	12 + 6 = 18	1 + 7 = 8	3 + 16 = 19	5 + 3 = 8	8 + 7 = 15
12 + 4 = 16	1 + 8 = 9	4 + 4 = 8	5 + 5 = 10	13 + 5 = 18	10 + 7 = 17
16 + 1 = 17	3 + 8 = 11	7 + 11 = 18	8 + 10 = 18	14 + 4 = 18	11 + 3 = 14

11. 3 → ↓ ↓ → → ↓ ↓ →

12.
- ● a ○ an mirror
- ● a ○ an bee
- ○ a ● an invitation
- ● a ○ an unicorn
- ● a ○ an jacket
- ● a ○ an frog
- ○ a ● an hourglass
- ● a ○ an comb
- ○ a ● an igloo
- ● a ○ an university
- ● a ○ an dog
- ● a ○ an bear
- ○ a ● an umbrella
- ○ a ● an eagle
- ● a ○ an horse
- ● a ○ an soap

13

1 2 3

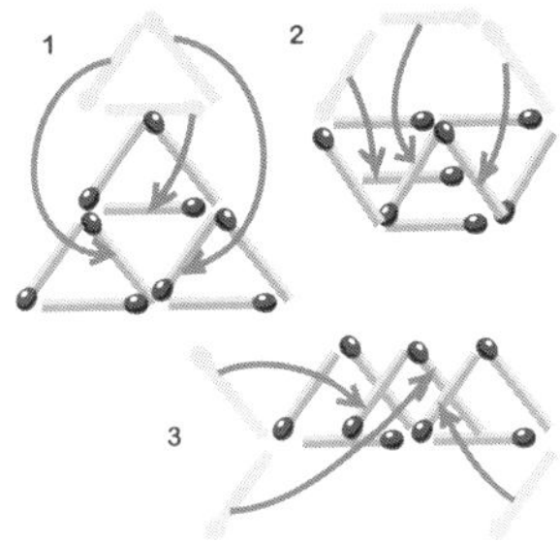

14

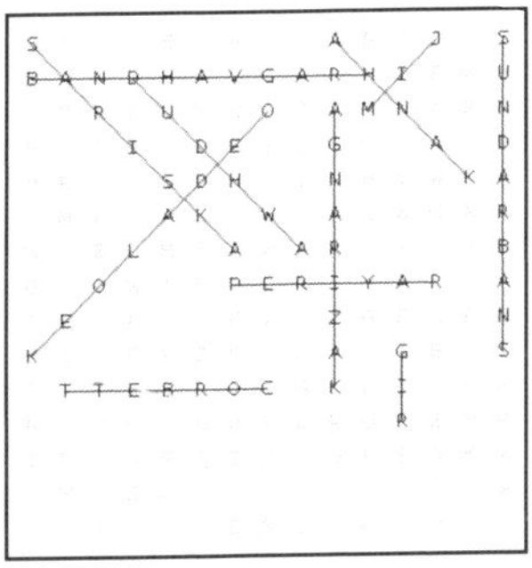

15

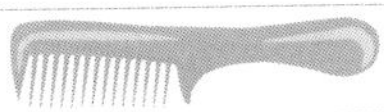

10.5 cm

10 cm

8.1 cm

11.4 cm

10.8 cm

3.5 cm

16

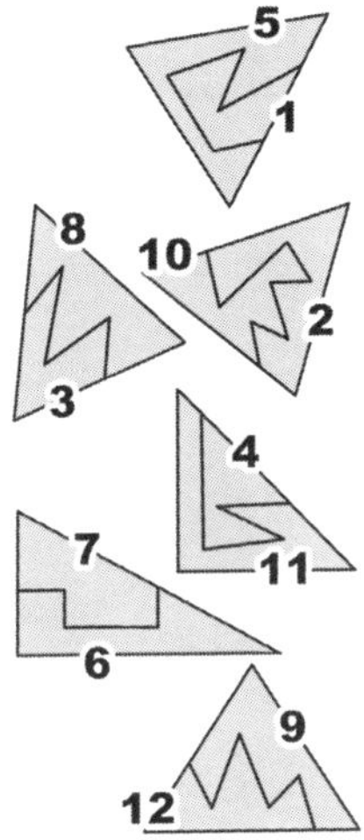

17

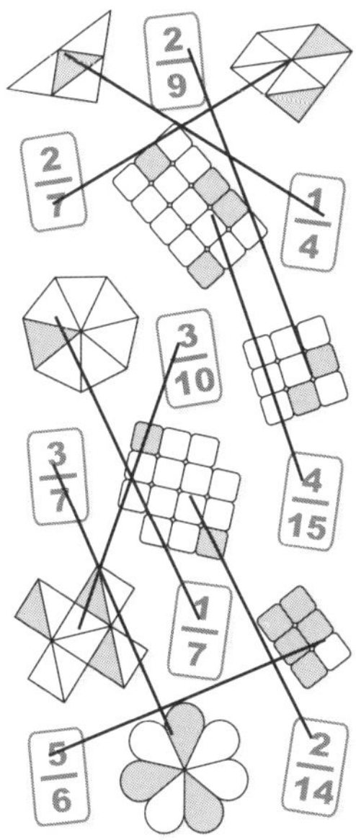

18 2.

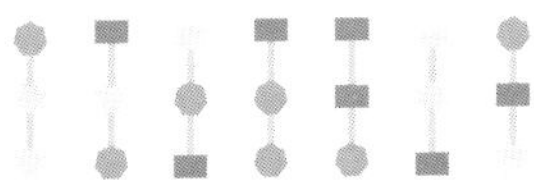

19

20 1-5 and 13-10

21

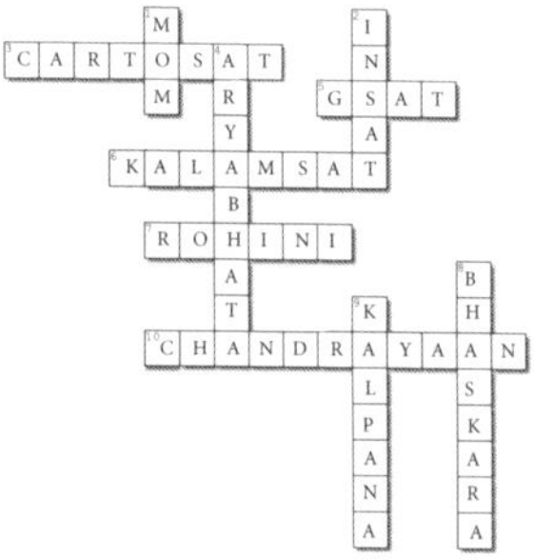

22

Facebook | Instagram | Twitter

LinkedIn | YouTube | Telegram

Vimeo | Snapchat | WhatsApp

23

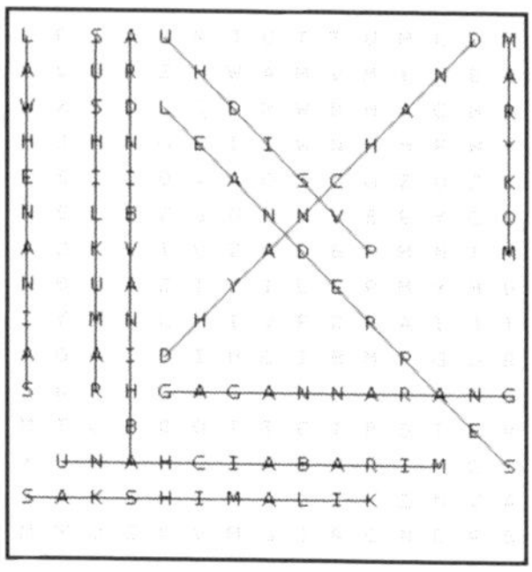

24

25

4	3	1	7	8	2	5	9	6
2	9	8	5	3	6	1	4	7
6	5	7	4	1	9	8	3	2
1	6	2	3	9	5	4	7	8
9	4	5	8	2	7	3	6	1
7	8	3	1	6	4	2	5	9
3	1	9	6	5	8	7	2	4
5	7	6	2	4	1	9	8	3
8	2	4	9	7	3	6	1	5

26 Umbrellas -9 | Clouds - 22 | Drop - 9 | Snowflakes - 11

27

1. Let off the hook
2. Caught red handed
3. To cry over spilt milk
4. To open a can of worms
5. It's a dog eat dog world
6. Cat got your tongue

28

29 10 (1-5, 2-9 and 8-12 are identical; 3-7 and 9-11 are mirror images)

30 Skier, Snowflake, Skating, Snowman, Vacations, Frost, Cold, Sledging, Icicles

31 Clockwise - 2, 8

Counterclockwise - 3, 4, 7, 10

32

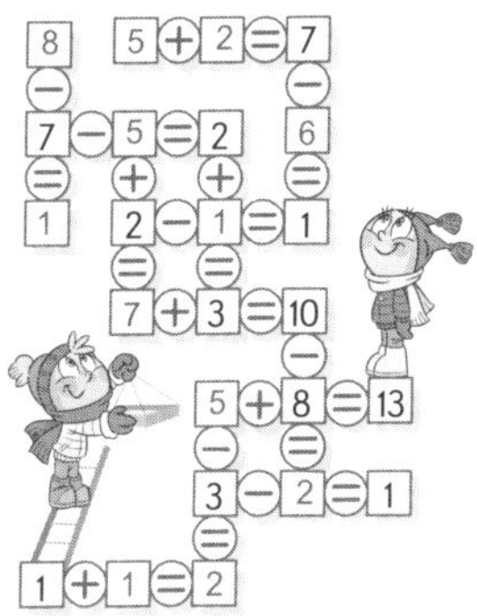

33

L	E	G	K	N	E	M	L	A	P
F	I	N	G	E	E	H	C	A	F
T	N	K	H	R	S	T	O	M	O
E	E	C	A	I	R	D	A	E	R
E	S	H	O	U	L	D	M	H	E
T	H	T	O	O	F	E	O	H	E
H	L	E	S	O	N	R	U	T	Y
E	I	P	E	Y	D	O	B	K	E
A	B	W	L	E	A	R	A	E	C
D	R	O	B	O	W	M	R	E	H

34

35 5.

36 1-K, 2-B, 3-I, 4-H, 5-G, 6-F, 7-E, 8-D, 9-C, 10-J, 11-A

37

BMW

TOYOTA

HONDA

JAGUAR

KIA

MERCEDES

FERRARI

TESLA

38

V − III = II

IV + I = V

VIII + I = IX

XI − X = I

X − V = V

XI = XX − IX

VII − V = I + I

39 8, 18

40 7

43

◺	□	○	△	▯	⬠
6	6	6	5	0	5

44

41

42

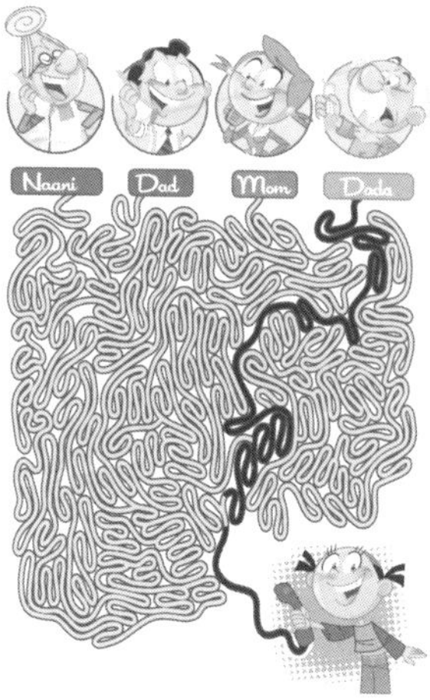

45

46. 6 - 1, 7 - 3, 8 - 5, 9 - 3, 10 - 4, 11 - 3, 12 - 2, 13 - 1, 14 - 2.

47. 20 bats

48.

49.

50.
1. Alexander Fleming
2. Antoine Lavoisier
3. Nikola Tesla
4. Louis and Auguste Lumière
5. Louis Pasteur
6. Thomas Edison
7. James Watt
8. Dmitri Ivanovich Mendeleev
9. Anton Van Leeuwenhoek
10. Alexander Graham Bell

51.

52.

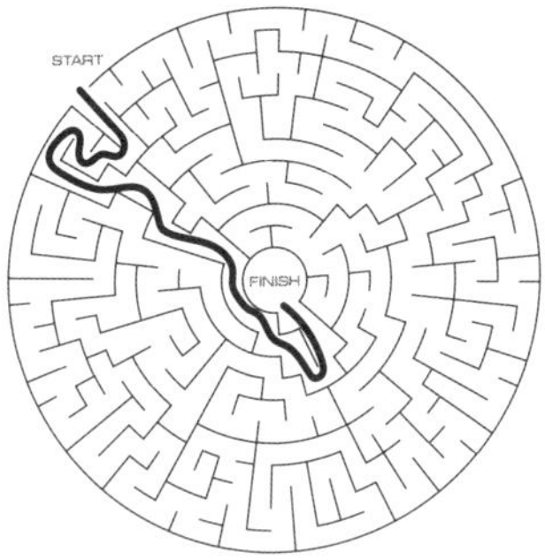

53.

6	6	7	6	6	6

54.

55.

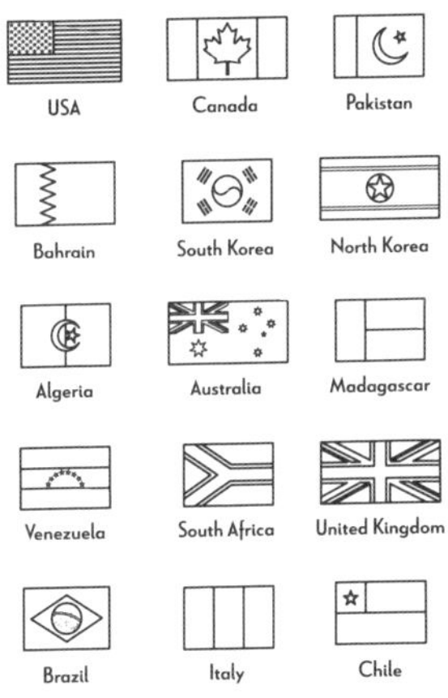

56. 1-20; 2-6 positive & 14 negative, 3-8 without head jewel, 4-6, 5-5, 6-2

57. 6

58. Clockwise - 2, 3, 4, 7, 8,
Counterclockwise - 6, 9

59. 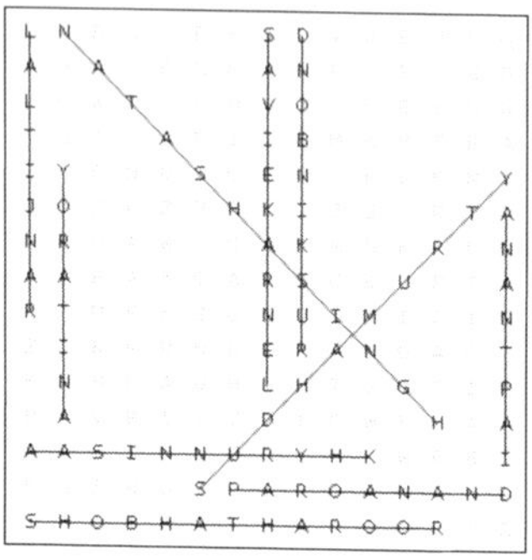

60. 62

61. Leopard, Whale, Panda,
Black Lemur, Polar Bear, Tiger

62. 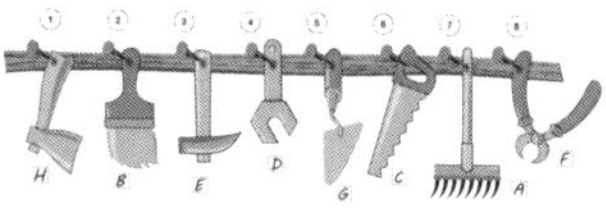

63.
1. Pretty please
2. Wish upon a star
3. Overseas travel
4. One in a million
5. Misunderstood
6. Think out of box

64. 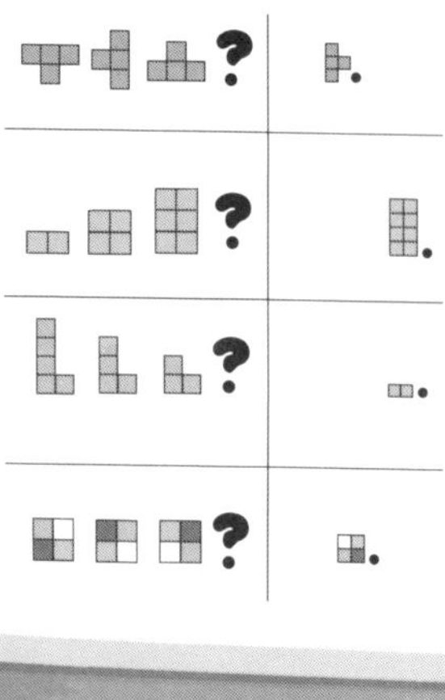

65.
1. Fatehpur Sikri
2. Mount Mary
3. Jantar Mantar
4. Konark Temple
5. Sanchi Stupa
6. Charminar
7. Salarjung Museum
8. Victory Tower
9. Hawa Mahal
10. Victoria Memorial

66.  02927546

67. 9 12

68. 

69. 

70 US - Dollar | China - Yuan | Saudi Arabia - Riyal | Cuba - Peso | Korea - Won | Brazil - Real | Israel - Shekel | Canada - Dollar

71 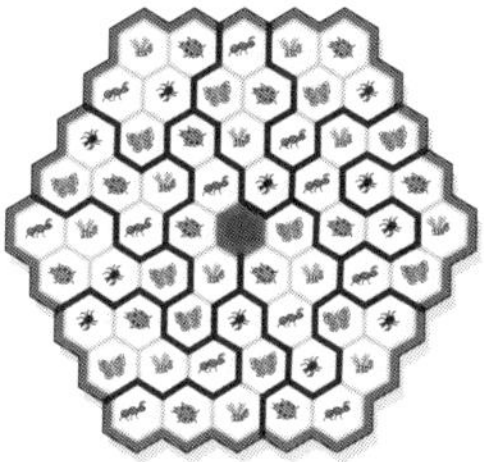

72 7, 9

73 1. Platypus | 2. Armadillo
3. Emu | 4. Aardvark
5. Hornbill | 6. Rhinoceros
7. Anteater | 8. Hippopotamus
9. Octopus

74 

75 

77 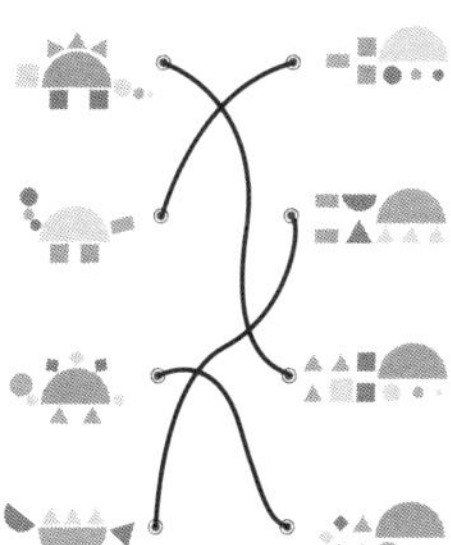

78 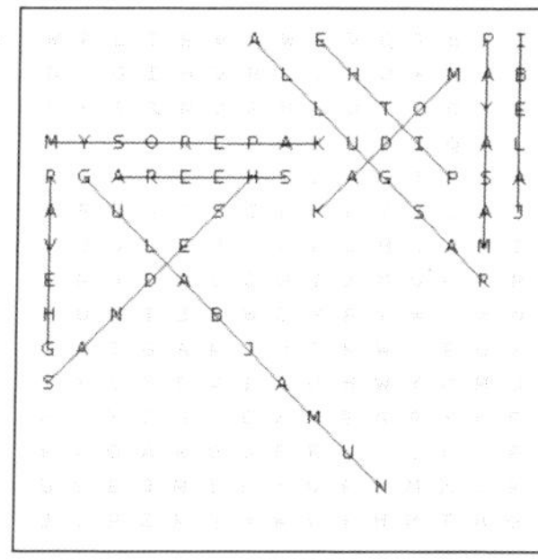

79 

80 1. You are under arrest
2. Breakfast
3. Top secret
4. Downhill
5. Nobody is above the law
6. Scrambled eggs

81 

82 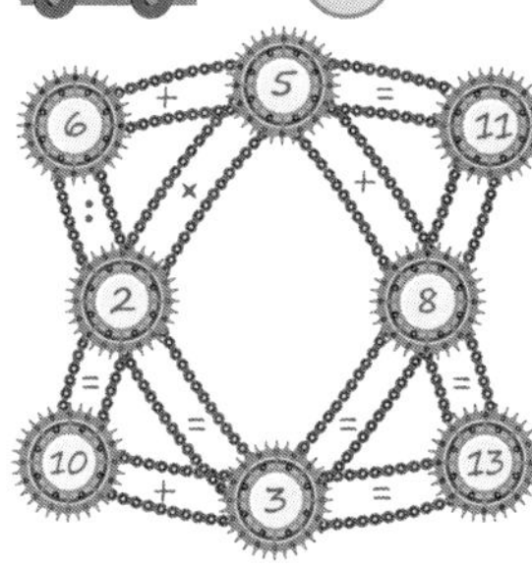

83

1 C 2 D 3 A 4 B

84

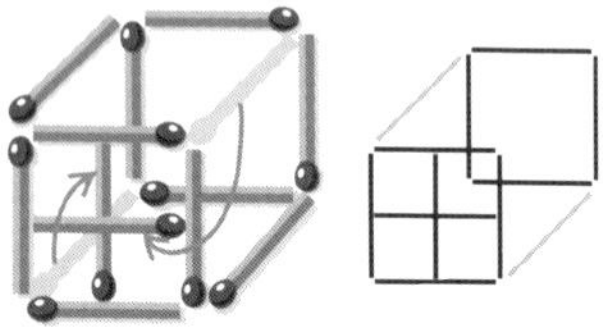

85

1. To sit on the fence
2. To pull someone's leg
3. Under the stars
4. Cool as cucumber
5. To spill the beans
6. To walk on thin ice

86

7  13 

87

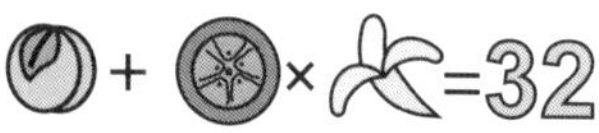

88

89

8	7	2	6	1	3	5	4	9
6	9	4	2	5	7	8	3	1
5	1	3	9	8	4	6	7	2
9	2	6	3	7	8	4	1	5
3	4	7	5	6	1	9	2	8
1	5	8	4	2	9	7	6	3
4	6	9	8	3	2	1	5	7
2	8	1	7	4	5	3	9	6
7	3	5	1	9	6	2	8	4

90

1-True
2-False (session at Lahore)
3-False (The Salt March was held from Sabarmati Ashram to Dandi)
4-True
5-False (The slogan 'Inquilab Zindabad' was given by Chandra Shekhar Azad)
6-False (Netaji Subhash Chandra Bose gave the slogan)
7-False (It was started by Mahatma Gandhi, in September 1920; Mangal Pandey spearheaded the Sepoy Mutiny of 1857, which is known as the step towards Indian Independence)
8-False (Moti Lal Nehru started The Independent)
9-False (It was A.O. Hume);
10-True

91

7 letter words
INMATES
FAMINES
6 letter words
FINEST
FAINTS
INFEST
5 letter words
FEAST
SAINT
MEANS
TAMES
4 letter words
SEAT
ITEM
MINT
SAME
EAST
NEST

92

94

1	3	5	7	9	11
1	2	4	8	16	32
1	2	3	5	8	13
9	7	5	3		1
8	4	2	1		1
12	15	18	111		114

95

.	.	.	D	.	A	R	C	B	.	.	.	.	.	.	.	.	.
.	.	.	U	.	.	.	.	E	.	.	.	.	.	.	C	.	.
.	.	.	S	.	.	.	.	L	.	.	.	C	H	E	A	P	B
C	.	.	T	P	.	.	.	O	.	.	.	.	R	.	R	.	O
I	.	.	Y	.	A	.	.	W	.	.	.	.	.	O	.	.	R
D	C	P	C	B	I	R	.	N	I	G	H	T	.	.	B	.	E
E	R	T	E	H	R	N	S	.	.	.	E	.	.	S	.	E	D
R	I	H	.	A	I	A	C	L	.	.	L	.	.	T	.	.	D
.	E	I	.	.	C	N	G	H	E	.	B	.	.	U	.	.	.
.	D	N	.	.	.	H	.	.	.	Y	O	.	.	D	.	.	.
.	.	G	G	R	A	B	.	.	.	.	W	.	.	Y	.	.	.
.	.	.	.	.	.	.	P	L	A	Y	E	R	S	.	.	.	.

96 1-17; 2-6; 3-9, 4-33

97

1. Broken promise | 2. Adverb
3. Growing economy
4. Jack in the box
5. Stand by me | 6. Belong

98

99

101

102

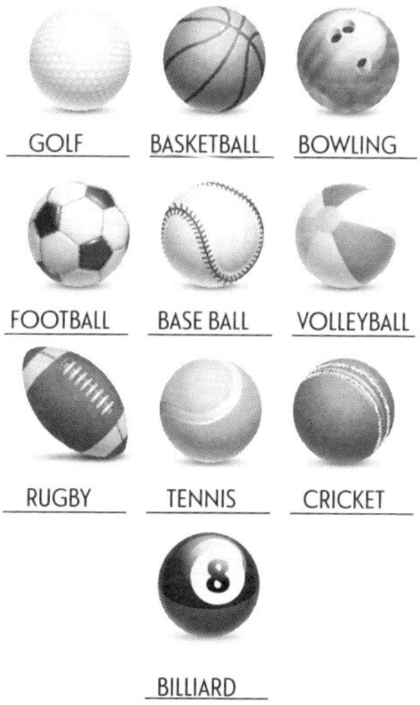

103 83

104

1. Egypt | 2. Palestine
3. Canada | 4. Norway
5. Japan | 6. Thailand
7. Switzerland | 8. Cuba

105 Kathak
Manipuri
Lavani
Mohiniyattam
Kalbeliya
Dhunuchi
Bharatnatayam

106
6♠ = (2)
6♥ = (5)
6♦ = (6)
6♣ = (10)

107
 4
 5
 8
 9
 12

108 (1) C (2) A (3) F (4) B
(5) D (6) E (7) H (8) G

109 1-I; 2-A; 3-E; 4-O; 5-M; 6-K; 7-F; 8-C; 9-D; 10-G; 11-N; 12-H ; 13-L; 14-J

110 1. 10, 2. 9, 3. 14, 4. 8, 5. 11, 6. 12, 7. 13